MW00856769

"I've decided to take your advice and face the facts, to be honest with myself and with you—as much as I can, as much as you can take." And with each phrase, each word, Adam's face moved fractionally, almost hesitantly, closer, until it filled her entire vision. Jennifer saw his eyelids close just before her own did, and then his lips closed gently upon hers.

In her limited experience she had never grown to think of any one man's kiss as very much different from another's. But Jennifer knew the moment Adam's lips met hers that this was different. It was as though there was something deep within the heart of every woman that lay dormant until it was awakened by the kiss of one very special man. And for her this was the kiss. And Adam Wilson was the man....

ABOUT THE AUTHOR

Rebecca Flanders is a native of Georgia who began her writing career at age nine. She completed her first novel by the time she was nineteen and sold her first book in 1979. Rebecca's hobbies are oil and watercolor painting and both composing and listening to music.

Books by Rebecca Flanders

HARLEQUIN AMERICAN ROMANCES

HARLEQUIN PRESENTS

These books may be available at your local bookseller.

For a list of all titles currently available,
send your name and address to:

Harlequin Reader Service
P.O. Box 52040, Phoenix, AZ 85072-2040
Canadian address: P.O. Box 2800, Postal Station A,
5170 Yonge St., Willowdale Ont. M2N 5T5

Second Sight

REBECCA FLANDERS

Harlequin Books

TORONTO • NEW YORK • LONDON
AMSTERDAM • PARIS • SYDNEY • HAMBURG
STOCKHOLM • ATHENS • TOKYO • MILAN

Published June 1984

First printing April 1984

ISBN 0-373-16058-5

Copyright © 1984 by Rebecca Flanders. All rights reserved.
Philippine copyright 1984. Australian copyright 1984.
Except for use in any review, the reproduction or utilization of
this work in whole or in part in any form by any electronic,
mechanical or other means, now known or hereafter invented,
including xerography, photocopying and recording, or in any
information storage or retrieval system, is forbidden without
the permission of the publisher, Harlequin Enterprises Limited,
225 Duncan Mill Road, Don Mills, Ontario, Canada M3B 3K9.

All the characters in this book have no existence outside the
imagination of the author and have no relation whatsoever to
anyone bearing the same name or names. They are not even
distantly inspired by any individual known or unknown to the
author, and all the incidents are pure invention.

The Harlequin trademarks, consisting of the words
HARLEQUIN AMERICAN ROMANCE, HARLEQUIN
AMERICAN ROMANCES, and the portrayal of a Harlequin,
are trademarks of Harlequin Enterprises Limited; the portrayal
of a Harlequin is registered in the United States Patent and
Trademark Office and in the Canada Trade Marks Office.

Printed in Canada

Chapter One

The inside of the tent smelled of sawdust, old camping trips, and a liberal dousing with Marianne Carter's musky perfume. Its location in the direct line of an ambivalent sun had kept the interior rather warm despite the chill of the October day that surrounded it, and the black cheesecloth draped on the walls gave a billowing effect of stifling intimacy. Jennifer Kiel contrasted the dusty, cramped interior with the bright carnival sights and sounds of the outdoors evident through the half-open back flap of the tent and wrinkled her nose in distaste. "Why don't *you* do it?" she complained to her sister, thinking hungrily of her missed lunch and the candy-apple concession her sister had dragged her unceremoniously away from not five minutes ago.

"You know I *would*..." Jo Ellen busily gathered up the folds of a voluminous black gauze cape and draped it over her sister's head. "But if I'm stuck in here the rest of the afternoon, who's going to keep the carny people from running away with the profits or the home-goods judges from getting soused on apple brandy or the greased pig from tearing through the mayor's platform?''

Jennifer giggled as she remembered the fiasco at last year's fair. Not only the greased pig, but an award-winning heifer, two cats, a dog, and the balky pony from the children's ride had conspired treason, and the ensuing stampede had ruined the baked goods display, the bandstand, the dried-flower arranging contest, and two old ladies with weak hearts. ''I don't know,'' countered Jennifer, still chortling helplessly with the memory, ''I thought the highlight of the day was seeing that pig in Mrs. Waldorp's wig.'' And then she yelped as her sister ruthlessly stuck her with a pin in an attempt to fasten the folds of the star-spangled cape over Jennifer's blue-jeaned figure. ''All right, all right.'' She scowled and held her arms straight out from her sides while Jo Ellen tried for a perfect fit of the garment, which would have easily held three of Jennifer. ''What happened to Marianne, anyway? Did someone find out she was playing with marked cards?''

''Little Sybil ate too many hot dogs,'' explained Jo Ellen patiently, inserting another pin into the front closure of the cape. ''And you don't use cards, just a little palm-reading and crystal-ball gazing. Hold still, will you?''

''This will never work,'' complained Jennifer, raising one arm high over her head so that the drooping pointed sleeve barely grazed the ground. ''Everyone will know it's me. Besides, I don't know how to be a fortune-teller.... What do I say?''

''Whatever comes into your scatter-brained

little head." Jo Ellen deftly draped a heavy black veil over her sister's distinctively colored strawberry hair and lowered a more transparent swatch of the material over her face. She stepped back to examine her critically. "You'll do, I suppose. You look mysterious enough. And so what, if anyone recognizes you? It's all in the spirit of fun."

"I feel like an idiot, that's what," retorted Jennifer, and registered one more protest as Jo Ellen firmly guided her to the chair behind the card table that was to be her home for the next three hours. "What do I *say*? Come on, Jo, you can't just leave me here—give me a script!"

"Just the usual," replied Jo Ellen with an airy wave as she parted the front flap for a peek at the festivities outside. "Romance, adventure, financial bounty, danger—anything that comes into your head. Will you look at that line! I told you this was the most popular booth here. Don't worry, Jen, you'll be fine, and Alice will relieve you at five. Good luck!"

Jennifer opened her mouth for another objection as her sister's cheerful countenance disappeared through the tent's flap, but all that came out was a smothered exclamation of pain as she started to rise and was stabbed by another pin. She comforted herself with a groan of resignation and then quickly composed her features into a mask of mystery and wisdom behind the sticky gauze veil as her first customer came in.

Adam Wilson had seen signs announcing various county fairs, harvest festivals, and Halloween carnivals throughout every state he had passed in his two-week tour of New England, and each one of them had seemed more compelling than the last. He did not know why he had never stopped. After all, the purpose of this trip had been to unwind, to take things at his own pace, to do exactly what he had wanted to do—with no one looking over his shoulder for once. No one had to tell him that he was still far from fulfilling his intentions at this point. "So big surprise," he muttered to his shaggy, silent companion in the front seat of the Blazer. "One more thing I can't do right. It takes a lot of talent to fail at taking a vacation, old boy, you've got to admit that...." He was ashamed of the self-pity in his voice and a little frightened by the realities that the self-pity was threatening to evoke, and with determination he clamped down on further indulgence. He pulled the Blazer to the curb directly underneath the orange-lettered banner that announced: "Southworth Township Carnival October 31st" and turned off the engine. The dog next to him pricked up his ears inquiringly, but settled back into the seat with a resigned grunt when Adam picked up his camera and got out.

The late afternoon sky was leaden and not particularly inspiring. He had rolls of undeveloped film depicting the same scenery on different landscapes—the quiet streets and the attractive storefronts, the stone courthouse, the white-steepled church in the distance. Was it true all New England towns looked alike, or was it simply that character, like beauty, was in the eye of the beholder? He only knew that he had two weeks

worth of picture postcards that weren't worth the
film they were printed upon and he was getting
tired of feeling sorry for himself.

He got back into the Blazer and slammed the
door with a vehemence that caused his companion, eminently attuned to his master's moods, to
sit up straight and begin to pant excitedly. Adam
ruffled his ears, grinned affectionately, and put
the vehicle into gear, following the signs to the
fairgrounds.

Neon colors, discordant sounds, and the tangy
odors of livestock and onion relish in the crisp fall
air sent him on a poignant sensory trip into childhood, and as the tires crunched to a stop upon the
graveled parking lot Adam felt a little like a child
again. A small Ferris wheel rotated in the distance, and the Scrambler gave off squeals and
shouts that faded and gathered with the ma-
chine's rotating motion and the whoosh of autumn air. Little goblins and ghosts, punk rockers
and space creatures, scampered across the parking
lot before him, chattering and giggling and tripping over the blowing folds of their costumes.
Beside him the dog began to whine and shift anxiously in his seat, ears alert and eyes eagerly seeking every detail of this new explosion of color and
activity, and Adam soothed him with an absent
stroke along his muzzle. "Sorry, old boy, you've
got a lot to learn about manners before I let you
out in a crowd this size. Take it easy; I won't be
long."

He got out and locked the door, pulling on a
flannel-lined jacket against the chill of the breeze

that lifted his hair and tingled new blood into his cramped fingers. On second thought he reached back inside and took his camera. Not that he was worried about leaving the expensive equipment in the vehicle—the guard inside would cheerfully divest any intruder who came within growling distance of an arm or a leg or both—but it occurred to him that if he was really serious about using this trip to get together some photos to send to Jake in New York this might be his best opportunity for subject matter yet. It also occurred to him that it was about time he stopped kidding himself and everyone else about the purpose of this trip and just admit that what he was really doing was running away.

By a quarter to five Jennifer was hot, sweaty, cramped, and starved. Her stomach growled ominously, and she looked with longing at the half-eaten caramel apple clutched in the grimy hand of her eight-year-old "customer," wondering whether or not the boy would accept a bribe from Madame Voltaire, Soothsayer to Princes, Kings, and Mystics of the Far East, for just one bite of the gooey, juicy fruit. Her client's disdainful comment decided her against asking. "You're not a fortune-teller," he announced scornfully, "you're Miss Kiel from the libary. Jimmy Johnson said you were a witch. I want my money back."

Repressing a long-suffering sigh and one last yearning glance at the dripping apple, Jennifer raised her arms in a slow, sweeping, dramatically threatening gesture and in an ominously deep voice replied, "I am Madame Voltaire, keeper of the secrets of the universe, and I turn red-haired little boys into toads with the blink of an eye."

"Blink," demanded the little boy obstreperously.

Jennifer sighed. "Get out of here, Derrick Grey, before I tell your mother that you're the one who painted Monica Castle's cat green last week."

The boy's eyes bulged. "How—how did you know that?" He gasped.

Jennifer smiled with satisfaction behind the veil, pleased that the eight-year-old mentality would not make the connection between the alleyway in which the dirty deed had been done and the library window that overlooked said alley. "Madame Voltaire knows all, sees all," replied Jennifer in her deep, commanding tones and with an imperious sweep of her arm. "Go."

As the visibly disturbed little boy stumbled back out into the daylight, Jennifer leaned back and rubbed her aching back, remonstrating with herself behind the wicked little smile of gratification that threatened to break through. Perhaps it had been a low blow to pull on a little kid, but she had been sitting here for almost three hours, and she was feeling a little punchy. She thought if she had to tell one more giggling teenage girl about the tall dark stranger she saw in the glass paperweight that served as a crystal ball she would scream. Besides, she thought with disgruntled self-justification, Derrick Grey had no business trying to blow her cover while eating a caramel apple right in front of her nose.

Jennifer groaned as she peeked surreptitiously at her watch and hoped Alice was not going to be late. Her phony predictions had begun to lose credibility about an hour ago when, out of a sense of mischief born of sheer boredom, she had told Dr. Brenner's aging widow to expect an illicit romantic encounter with a blue-eyed Italian gypsy and sent the primly scandalized eighty-six-year-old woman from the tent in a confusion of blushes and giggles. Since then she had kept herself entertained by making up all sorts of unlikely stories, including a veiled warning to the good-looking young Methodist minister to be cautious in his dealings with a certain red-haired librarian. She knew she was headed for trouble if she didn't curb her instinct for teasing, but so far all her patrons had left satisfied with having gotten their dollar's worth of entertainment, and besides, the minister had known it was Jennifer behind the veil and had enjoyed the flirtation.

She looked up hopefully as the tent flap parted again, but relief turned to disappointment as the angular patch of light silhouetted a figure too tall and too slim to be Alice. When the dropping flap obscured the glare and reduced the tent once more to dusty twilight, Jennifer's rapidly adjusting eyes told her that the figure was a man. That was a surprise, because most of her patrons had been teenage girls and boys under the age of ten, and further, this man was a complete stranger. This was not to imply that she knew by name everyone who graced the fairgrounds today, but most of the adults who had stopped by her tent had done so specifically because they knew she was playing the role of Madame Voltaire and had come in to let her know that they knew. Geared up for a challenge, Jennifer assumed her most mysterious air and determined to give this stranger his money's worth—her final performance before her relief came.

He paused politely before the straight-backed chair on the opposite side of the black-draped table and inquired in a pleasant masculine drawl, "Madame Voltaire, I presume?"

Jennifer looked for a moment into eyes as grey as the heavy slate sky outside and almost forgot her line. It was one thing doing this nonsense for giggly teenagers and amused friends and neighbors, but the presence of this male stranger within the intimate confines of the tent suddenly made her nervous. She recovered her composure quickly, however, and with an airy wave of her arms and much billowing of black crepe she commanded throatily, "Have a seat, my child."

She choked back a giggle at the amused lift of an eyebrow her words provoked and had to once again firmly rescue her composure. The yards of black material could do little to convince anyone that the woman behind it was old enough to be calling anyone nearer to thirty than twenty "my child." He arranged his lean frame in the small chair across the table from her and waited, his face composed into studious lines.

The tent was lit by two artificial candles wired to

the canvas walls, and Jennifer's vision had grown accustomed to the dimness and to the black veil that obscured her eyes. She had no trouble at all observing her customer while, presumably, remaining unobserved herself. His hair was a muddy blond, shaggy at the collar and cut thick over the forehead from a side part. In the deceptive interior light it took on a tinny cast, almost the color of his eyes. His eyes were wide-set and lightly fringed, his nose delicately formed over a pleasant, expressive mouth. His cheekbones, too, were arched in an expression of delicate bone structure, and their prominence gave his face an almost hollow look, as though he had recently lost weight. His complexion was very fair, almost pallid, bespeaking a man who very rarely got out of doors. It was a vulnerable face at first glance, easily likeable and empathetic. But Jennifer did not miss the tracing of a sharp line between his brows that suggested this man was fond of scowling, or perhaps worrying, and there were other lines, sharper and more distinct, near his mouth that would look grim when accentuated. Those were marks of distance and suffering, not disguised by the pleasant, lighthearted demeanor he wore for this occasion, and Jennifer could not help wondering what raw hands life had dealt him to put such scars on an otherwise beautiful face.

She had not noticed how much time had passed while she made these assessments, and she was embarrassed when he prompted helpfully, "Shall I cross your palm with silver?"

She glanced at him quickly from behind the pro-

tective veil and realized that while she had been
studying him, he had also been scrutinizing her.
What he could have seen to put that look of
amused tolerance in his eyes she did not know,
but she decided it was time to put daydreams aside
and get down to business.

"Give me your hand," she commanded huski-
ly.

"Better yet," he murmured, and extended his
hand.

The moment their fingers touched blue sparks
crackled against the black background of the table.
Jennifer gave an undignified squeak, "Ouch!" and
withdrew her hand, rubbing her fingertips and
peering at him suspiciously. There was surprise in
his eyes too, but also a sparkle of amusement, and
he apologized blandly. "Sorry. Crepe-soled shoes
and static electricity. Shall we try it again?"

Jennifer took his hand cautiously—no shock this
time—and opened it palm upward between both
of hers. His hand was large between her small,
delicate ones, soft and uncallused, as smooth and
fair as his face. Its light skin was marred by an
even lighter circle on the third finger of his left
hand, and Jennifer thought she understood something of what had caused the lines of unhappi-
ness on his face. It was the scar of a wedding
band recently removed. She suddenly felt a deep
empathy for this lonely stranger with the warm,
fragile hand and the vulnerable face; she found
herself wishing they had met differently. She said
softly, "I see tragedy in your past; heartbreak
and war within the home." The tensing of his

arm muscle and the slight curling of his fingers told her she had hit it right on the mark, as of course she had known she would. It did not take any particular gift of insight to tell her this was a man suffering badly from the breakdown of a marriage. "You are struggling under a weight of guilt for something that cannot be changed, blaming yourself for circumstances beyond your control."

Now his hand tightened as though to draw away, and he said briefly, "Do you double as a psychiatrist?"

She knew she had gone too far when she looked up and saw the sharp line between his brows. The eyes were troubled and stormy. And of course he was right. He had come here for fun and entertainment; she had no right to remind him of what he was trying to escape from. Instinctively she tightened her hand on his to prevent his withdrawal, and she saw a surprised softening in his eyes at her touch. Slowly his hand relaxed, and she knew she had been given a second chance.

She was inordinately grateful for the smoothing of that troubled line between his brows. All right: light and easy from now on. She would give him his five minutes' worth of fantasy and more. "Aha," she said, studying the pinkish network of lines on his palm, "but things are looking up." She strained to remember what Jo had told her: finances, romance, adventure. "I see immediate improvement in your financial affairs. Unexpected windfall profits from an anonymous source."

"Now, that's more like it," he agreed in satisfaction, leaning back so that his long arm stretched the length of the table and his jacket fell open to reveal a lean breadth of chest covered in a plaid flannel. "Was that your little boy who left just before I came in?"

She was startled. "No. Why?"

He shrugged, watching her. "His red hair."

She stared at him. "How did you know I had red hair?"

He grinned. "Your veil is slipping."

Her free hand fluttered to repair her veil while she struggled beneath an unexpected blush to regain control of the encounter. This was really silly. She had *told* Jo it was silly.... Jennifer took a deep breath, concentrated on his palm, and gathered all her imaginative resources. He had not paid a dollar at the door to have cocktail conversation with her. She plunged back into her role. "Ah... I see danger." She proceeded to borrow liberally from a television program she had watched last night. "A climbing accident... mountain steppes... a large black animal. A bear." She glanced at him in satisfaction, but he seemed unimpressed.

"Do you get many bears in the mountains around here?" he inquired casually.

She tried not to scowl at him. Not only was the nearest mountain range some distance away, but the last she had heard, the type of bear she had in mind was threatened with extinction. His look told her he knew it. He was definitely not entering into the spirit of the game.

"I see you standing at the crossroads of opportunity," she went on doggedly, "and the course you take will change the rest of your life." That was always good. Just the right amount of vague coupled with ethereal wisdom.

He inquired curiously, "Are you married, Madame Voltaire?"

Her heart skipped a beat, and she had to quickly bite back an automatic reply, remembering her role. She deliberately and forcefully smoothed back the long fingers that threatened to curl around hers, and the tent suddenly seemed much too small, and much too private, for the two of them.

Staring him down through the gauzy veil, she said, "I see romance coming into your life."

"I love it," he murmured, and his eyes held her in teasing provocation. "Go on, pray do."

"A brief, poignant encounter," she finished deliberately. "With a hairy dwarf."

The spark of laughter in his eyes showed he had a sense of humor even as he drawled meaningfully, "Is that the best you can do?"

She withdrew her hand as once again his fingers began to close around hers. She folded her hands primly in her lap and replied solemnly, "Indeed, sir, it is."

He lifted an eyebrow and inquired, "Does this mean my dollar's worth of hand-holding is up?"

She inclined her head once, sagely, and he rose lazily. "Right." He smiled down at her and she was amazed by the transformation in his face when he smiled. He should always smile. "I'll be sure to watch out for mountain bears and hairy dwarfs. Thanks for the tip.''

"It comes with the price of admission," she told him, responding so easily to his smile that she forgot to use her "Madame Voltaire" voice. He acknowledged the fact with another quick smile, looking at her for just a moment longer than was strictly necessary, searching her face behind the veil and making her blush again. Then he turned and left.

Adam paused for a moment outside the tent and let his eyes adjust to the fading gray day. There was a smile of reminiscence on his face, and he was convinced that stopping here today was the one and only right thing he had done in the past year—perhaps in his whole life. He had not felt so free since he was a kid.

And then the smile altered with disturbed puzzlement as he thought about the girl inside the tent. He had seen nothing of her except a pair of tiny white hands and a shadowy face, and yet... He was telling himself not to be an idiot and deciding it might be time to start moving on when a sudden gust of wind blew a scrap of paper against his jeaned leg and plastered it there. He bent to brush it off, then straightened up slowly, a dollar bill between his fingers. A quizzical smile tugged at his lips as he glanced over his shoulder at the tent he had just vacated. Windfall profits? He glanced dutifully around for the possible loser of the money, but of course it was futile. The smile gave way to a grin as he tucked the bill into his front pocket and sauntered away. It did appear as though his luck were changing.

When Jennifer came out, it was that spooky time of day just before sunset but not quite dusk; the sun could not seem to make up its mind whether to linger or to go. The light had a grainy appearance as it seeped away in barely measurable portions, visibility was impaired, and everything seemed just a little unreal, as though life were being viewed through a dusty windowpane. Jennifer had been half awed by this time of day since she was a child, yet it was her favorite time. Anything seemed possible in this netherland where the dying sun and the encroaching darkness combined forces to spread their granules of mystery over the landscape, and the last few minutes of the day held a potent promise.

All over the fairgrounds bright lights twinkled and blinked and rotated, and Jennifer tried not to look at them. She knew it was dangerous to do so, but like the uncertain twilight the shocking flash of red and blue and neon yellow held an exciting compulsion for her. Like the moth to the flame, she thought absently, and deliberately turned her eyes toward the less harmful fascination of the colorful jostling crowd that passed before her while she paused to get her bearings.

She must have stood there longer than she realized, trying to decide whether to appease her gnawing hunger with a wide variety of carnival treats—the mingled aromas of which were a powerful temptation—or to go home and make herself a more nutritious meal. Suddenly her arm was gripped tightly and Phillip's concerned face filled her vision. "Jenny, are you all right?" he demanded.

She scowled irritably at her brother-in-law and pulled her arm away. "Don't sneak up on me like that—you scared me to death!"

Worry still creased Phillip's face as he peered at her suspiciously. "You were just standing there, staring . . . I told Jo you had no business working this afternoon!"

"For goodness' sake, Phil," she exclaimed in exasperation. "You're worse than a mother!"

He seemed far from reassured. "You look tired. I'll take you home. And on the way, I want to talk to you about seeing Dr. Thompson again."

Jennifer was incredibly grateful for the sound of a masculine voice behind her. "Well, well, if it isn't Madame Voltaire, Soothsayer to Kings, Princes, and Mystics of the Far East."

She turned with a smile of relief and welcome and was surprised to see the amused gray eyes of her last customer. She said, somewhat taken aback, "H-hello! How did you know it was me?"

"Second sight," he assured her gravely. "Did you really think you were the only gypsy on the premises?"

"I see," she replied in appropriately sober tones. "I'm honored to meet one of my own kind."

Phillip, ever vigilant, cleared his throat behind her, hinting for an introduction. That, of course, presented something of a problem, but Jennifer did her best. "This is my sister's husband, Phillip Pierce. Phil, this is—"

"Adam Wilson," the stranger said, rescuing her gallantly, and extended his hand. "I was just passing through and couldn't resist stopping. Didn't I see your name on one of the storefronts in town?"

"Why, yes," Phillip replied, immediately interested in a prospective client. "Real estate. Are you thinking of stopping with us?"

"I'm afraid not. This was just an unscheduled visit to capture the local color."

Jennifer noticed for the first time the expensive-looking camera around his neck and inquired, "Are you a professional photographer?"

"Yes," he answered briefly, and Jennifer received the impression that she had somehow offended him. Before she could analyze this reaction, however, the pleasant mask was back over his features and he suggested, "I was hoping you would be interested in sharing the results of an unexpected windfall profit from an anonymous source." He pulled a dollar bill from his front pocket and waved it before her. "Blew right into my hand the minute I left you. Nice trick; you'll have to tell me how you do it."

She giggled. "That's against union rules."

"Jennifer," Phillip said meaningfully, "we really should get going. ..."

Jennifer hesitated for just a moment. Under other circumstances she never would have considered going off with a stranger at a fair, but Phillip badly needed to be taught a lesson. She smiled at the man called Adam Wilson and said, "How much junk food do you suppose that dollar will buy at a place like this?"

"It won't take long to find out," he replied, and touched her shoulder lightly to lead her away. Jennifer spared just one smug glance for her scowling brother-in-law, before she began to wind her way through the crowd with Adam Wilson by her side. He was silent, and Jennifer began to wonder whether he was regretting his impulsive invitation. To forestall a developing awkwardness she demanded brightly, "So how did you really recognize me?"

He grinned at her and the atmosphere between them no longer seemed awkward. "That hair of yours is pretty hard to miss," he pointed out. "But of course, this"—unexpectedly he brushed the tip of her chin with his finger—"was the real giveaway. I don't imagine there are too many women with a birthmark like that in the world, much less at a small-town fair."

The surprising touch of his finger left her skin tingling, perhaps for no other reason than that it was unexpected. She covered her confusion with a grimace and a self-deprecating shrug. "My grandmother called it an angel's kiss, my mother called it a beauty mark. I call it just plain ugly."

The blemish to which she referred was a very pale beige tear-shaped mark in the center of her pointed chin, the only remarkable feature in an otherwise perfectly ordinary pixie-shaped face. Jennifer had never been self-conscious about it, but neither had she ever grown to like it, con-

sidering the birthmark just another feature of a
prosaic little body that would never be beautiful,
glamorous, or interesting—just functional. Her
eyes were another mismatch for her coloring,
golden brown when they should have been green
or hazel, and there was not a freckle on her body,
which led most people to believe her hair color
was artificially obtained. Her neck was too long for
her small, triangular face, and throughout adolescence she had been all arms and legs, tall and
skinny. Her figure was slim and boyish. Her one
distinguishing feature was her long, smooth hair
in its gleaming orange-gold color, but, worn loose
and straight as it was, it did nothing to detract
from the overall impression she gave of being a
slightly mischievous teenager.

He was looking at her seriously, studying her
face, and just before the point at which his scrutiny would become embarrassing, he decided,
"Character. It gives your face character. I like it."

She grimaced and shrugged to hide the sudden
pleasure at his compliment, and she touched his
arm to lead him toward the line that had formed
in front of a concession booth. "I wasn't fishing
for compliments."

"And I wasn't giving them," he replied easily.
"Were you born around here?"

"Um-hmm. What about you?"

"Hawaii."

She laughed up at him in astonishment. "Come
on, you're kidding! No one is *born* in Hawaii!"

"I was," he assured her. There was an easy,
friendly light in his eyes, and the troubled lines on

his face were only memories. It occurred to Jennifer that this was a man who was more comfortable being happy than sad, and it was more of an effort for him to be tense than relaxed. It was hard not to like him, easy to feel comfortable with him.

"My father was stationed at Pearl Harbor," he explained. "Of course, we went back to the States a few months later. I've never been back."

"You'll have to go home someday to trace your roots," she suggested gravely.

His eyes twinkled. "That I will."

They decided on a paper bowl filled with taco chips and a spicy hot nacho cheese sauce, and Jennifer dug into the gooey mixture with relish while Adam purchased a large bag of unbuttered, unsalted popcorn.

"So where are you on your way to now?" Jennifer inquired as they started walking away.

"Canada, eventually." His eyes twinkled as he glanced down at her. "You sure do ask a lot of questions for a fortune-teller."

"Ah, but I see only into the future," she replied in a suitably mysterious tone, "not into the past."

"Convenient," he agreed.

She realized that what she had assumed to be an aimless walk had led them away from the center of activity and toward the parking lot. She started to turn back toward the safety of the crowd, but he stopped her. "Come on." He placed his hand on her elbow and gestured toward the dimly lit parking lot. "I want to show you something."

Sure you do, thought Jennifer with an ugly suspicion she did not really believe, and his eyes laughed as he read her thoughts.

"Do you envision a mugging or a rape in your future?" he teased, pausing while she made up her mind.

She shrugged in what she hoped was a display of nonchalance. "Let's just say we small-town girls aren't as dumb as we look. Cardinal rule number one: Never be bribed by a bowl of nacho chips into following a strange man into a dark parking lot."

He sighed dramatically. "Foiled again! The old nacho-chip routine—I should have known better than to trust it." She tried not to giggle, and he explained, "See that blue truck over there? Right beside the parking attendant with the flashlight? I have to go check something inside; I'll be right back."

Cardinal rule number two: Always trust your instincts. Besides, what could happen with a parking attendant standing six feet away? With only a moment's hesitation she followed him.

He waited for her beside the truck, as though he had had no doubt she would follow. There was a look of amusement on his face she did not understand as he said sardonically, "Meet the large black animal you saw in my future. His name is Bear."

He stepped away from the window and Jennifer gave a gasp of delight, not fear, at the huge black muzzle that poked its way eagerly through the small crack between window and door frame.

"What a beautiful dog!" she exclaimed. "Is his name really Bear? He sure looks like one, doesn't he?"

"Come on, lady, the gag is up." There was laughter in his voice, but also a rueful sort of admiration. "There can't have been too many men with Newfoundland dogs here today, and you must have heard me use his name when I drove up. Clever though." He opened the door and warned over his shoulder, "Stay back now. He's vicious with strangers."

"Are you suggesting," declared Jennifer indignantly as Adam opened the bag of popcorn and spread it on the floor for his enthusiastic pet, "that I cheated? How could I? I was in that tent all afternoon, and I've never seen this dog before. Hey there, fellow, you're a real beauty, aren't you?"

"Watch it!" There was real alarm in Adam's face as she leaned over him to stroke the dog, and he started to jerk her arm away. "I told you—"

But he broke off in amazement as the dog, far from biting Jennifer's hand, actually looked up from the popcorn feast to lick it. He stepped back wordlessly as the animal, beneath Jennifer's gentle coaxing, ignored the popcorn altogether, sat up on the seat, placed his front paws on her shoulders, and began to lick her face. Jennifer accepted the cheerful greeting with laughter and welcome for a moment, ruffling his shaggy coat and burrowing her face into the fur; then she said, "All right, fellow, that's enough. Finish your supper."

Obediently the dog returned to the popcorn.

It was a moment before Adam could speak, and then it was only to utter a soft, 'I'll be damned.'' He stared at her suspiciously. "How did you do that? That dog is trained to attack first and think later; that's why I can't take him out in crowds. He won't respond to any command but my own. How did you do it?''

She shrugged and stuffed her fingers into the front pockets of her jeans, watching the dog. "Animals like me. It's a gift.''

He looked at her for a moment longer, warily. "It must be your perfume," he decided at last.

She gave him an amused glance. "You are a skeptic, aren't you?''

"Mostly," he agreed, and locked the door.

"Well, we'll just have to change that," she declared mischievously. "All skeptics turn into pumpkins on Halloween night.''

There was warmth in his gray eyes as he looked from her back to the colorful lure of the landscape they had just left. "This is wild, isn't it?" he said, and his eyes were sparkling like a boy's as he looked back to her. "Do you have any idea how long it's been since I've been on a Scrambler?''

"Fifteen years?" she suggested.

"Close." There was provocative laughter in his eyes. "I stole my first kiss on one.''

"That must have been quite an experience!''

"Unforgettable," he assured her, and when he took her hand it seemed like the most natural thing in the world. "Let's see if I can remember my technique.''

He did not kiss her on the Scrambler, nor the Ferris wheel, nor the Rocket Ship.... In fact, it was not until he had lost three dollars at the dart-throwing game that he remembered to ask her name. Jennifer felt as comfortable and relaxed with him as if he was an old childhood friend— more so, because, knowing nothing about her, he accepted her for exactly what she appeared to be and it was good to relax and be herself with someone. Adam too, was relaxed into what she had initially guessed was his natural condition. He had such an innate ability to enjoy life she wondered again what had put those lines of stress on his face she had seen when they had first met.

It was on the steps of Horror Mountain—a permanent display operated every year by the Jaycees—that he first put his arm around her. It was a very natural gesture, for the cold night air was penetrating Jennifer's sweater, and he could not help but notice she was beginning to shiver. Yet Jennifer was unprepared for the wonderful sensation the warmth of his arm around her shoulders sent spreading throughout her whole body, the way it made her heart speed just the slightest and her cheeks tingle. It made her want to snuggle close to him and stay that way for a long time, and that shocked her. She had never before considered herself an indiscriminately affectionate person, and this man was a total stranger. She thought she should pull away, but she didn't. Instead she glanced at him shyly, wondering whether he was experiencing the same feelings.

Apparently not, for his smile was totally noncommittal as he commented, "You must be freezing. Here, take my jacket."

She protested as he shrugged out of his jacket, but he insisted with a grin, "Indulge me. The last time I saw a girl wearing my jacket I was a senior in high school, and this is a night for revisiting childhood, isn't it?"

She pushed her arms into the long sleeves of the jacket, laughing at the way it draped over her hands and almost touched her knees, and for just a moment there was an affectionate light in his eyes that caught her off guard. For one crazy moment she thought he might actually lean down and kiss her, and the laughter died in sudden anticipation in her throat. But the moment was gone before it had even been born.

A group of laughing, shouting boys burst between them, pushing Jennifer against the rail. Adam was standing with one foot on the edge of the upper step, and when he was shoved he lost his balance; only Jennifer's quick supporting arm prevented his knee from striking the step. She demanded quickly, "Are you all right?" and he straightened up slowly, a peculiar expression on his face.

"An accident on the mountain steps?" he commented dryly. "Really, Madame Voltaire."

She laughed out loud in delight. "Hey, I am good, aren't I? See what you get for being skeptical?"

"I think you bribed those kids," he told her mildly, and once again his arm slipped around her waist. "Let's find something less exciting to do; I suddenly have a feeling that the monsters inside Horror Mountain might be real.''

Jennifer began to hum a spooky tune under her breath and then laughed at the pained expression on his face.

He bought cones of blue cotton candy and held her hand as they wandered about from one display to the other, finally stopping within the small circle that had gathered around the organ grinder and his monkey. "Where are you from?" Jennifer asked after a time of easy silence between them.

"Chicago," he answered briefly, and pinched off a bit of the fluffy candy.

Jennifer had long since realized that he was not going to volunteer any information about his past and that, in fact, the subject seemed almost taboo. That was frustrating because Jennifer wanted to know everything about him—who he was, what he did, what had happened to his marriage, what had put those lines of suffering on his face. And of course that was ridiculous, because he was just a stranger passing through, one whom she would never see again after tonight but one who, in some inexplicable way, had suddenly become very important to her. So she tried again. "You're a long way from home, aren't you?"

He changed the subject. "You people sure put on a show for a small-town fair. Do you know I've been all over the United States, and this is the first time in all my thirty-six years I've actually seen a real organ-grinder's monkey?"

The organ grinder was actually a farmer who

lived some ten miles out of town and who was forgiven his eccentric taste in pets purely because of the entertainment he provided on occasions such as this. The monkey was a rhesus named Cerisse that Jennifer had known since she had first been rescued from a medical laboratory upstate. Struck by a sudden sense of mischief, Jennifer knelt down and snapped her fingers invitingly. The organ grinder, recognizing her, released the leash, and Cerisse scampered into her arms.

Adam laughed and turned to pet the monkey, but he stopped laughing when Cerisse returned his greeting enthusiastically, wrapping her arms about his neck and covering his face with wet, exuberant kisses.

Jennifer doubled over with laughter at his startled exclamations and futile attempts to dislodge his amorous visitor; his cotton candy dropped on the ground and he twisted his face this way and that to no avail—escape was impossible. The delighted crowd laughed and cheered him on, and Jennifer, gasping and wiping away tears, managed at last, "There's—your brief romantic encounter with—a hairy dwarf!" She dissolved into laughter again at his glare.

At last, however, taking pity on him, she pried the monkey loose and sent her scampering back to her master. Adam, scrubbing his face with a handkerchief, declared darkly, "You *are* a witch—and an underhanded one at that! I know you bribed that monkey!"

Jennifer shook her head, still chortling helplessly. "Cerisse has a weakness for cotton candy," she told him, her eyes dancing. "And you"—she touched his face lightly, near his lips—"had it all over your face!"

Something softened in his eyes at her touch, and she saw a deep glow of awareness that made her breath catch and her heart skip. He said softly, "I still think you're a witch." She dropped her hand and turned to walk beside him with a casualness she did not feel.

Yet something seemed to have changed in the atmosphere around them as they walked through the thinning crowds, watching one booth after another close up. He did not touch her, but there was an acute awareness between them, a lingering expectation, a new interest. Jennifer found it hard to believe that he would leave in a few minutes and she would never see him again. The evening they had spent together felt like a beginning, but it was in reality an ending. They were strangers, and they had shared no more than a few hours of light fun, yet Jennifer did not feel as though they were strangers, and she did not want it to end. Once again she ventured a glance at the blinking lights of the Ferris wheel, but looked away just as the hollow feeling began to form in her stomach. The compulsion she was beginning to feel for this man was very much like that which prompted her to look at the lights when she knew she shouldn't— it was unwise and irrational, but powerful nonetheless.

He interrupted her reverie with a casual inquiry. "Are you really a psychic?"

She smiled and tucked her hands into the

overly large pockets of his jacket for warmth. "No," she admitted. "My grandmother was, though. She predicted the sinking of the Titanic."

"Aha, so witchery runs in your family," he teased her. "Dangerous business this close to Salem." Then, "Will you disappear if I try to take your picture?"

She laughed. "Should I?"

"It's a well-known fact," he assured her soberly, taking up his camera, "that witches, demons, ghosts, and other mysterious personages cannot be captured on film. Let's give it the acid test, shall we?"

She threw up her hands in laughing protest as she began to click the shutter. "Unfair! You won't get anything on that film even if I'm not a witch—you're not using a flash!"

"Don't have to," he replied, angling closer for a variety of shots. "The camera compensates with natural light. Stop giggling; try to look mysterious."

"Sorry," she retorted, pushing up her hair and giving him an exaggerated profile. "Sexy is the best I can do."

He grinned as he looked up. "You do that just fine."

She was glad the night air hid her blush, and she dropped her arms, commenting casually, "You haven't taken any pictures all night. What suddenly gave you the bug?"

"I didn't see anything worth photographing," he answered, and he smiled as he let the camera fall again to his chest. "Until now."

There was that meaningful light in his eyes again as he came over to her, and once again her chest tightened in anticipation. She could not have imagined the subtle intent there as his eyes traveled slowly over her face, touching on her eyes, her nose, her lips, the birthmark on her chin, and then again to her lips. And there was no controlling the nervous, unsure response generated in her own senses as he half lifted his hand as though to touch her. But then it was gone.

His eyes left her to wander over the dimming landscape about them, his hand resting easily by his side again. She might have imagined the entire episode. "Looks like they're closing up on us," he remarked. "I guess I'd better be on my way."

Jennifer swallowed back an acute and very irrational disappointment as she responded lightly, "Going to make Canada tonight?"

"No." He smiled as he looked at her. "But I should be thinking about a motel or a campground somewhere along the road. I don't suppose this charming little burg has any of those commodities?"

"I'm afraid not," replied Jennifer, her disappointment mounting. She shrugged out of his jacket and held it out to him, trying to smile. "Thanks for the use of the jacket."

He seemed reluctant to take the jacket, as though he, too, was aware that the gesture was symbolic of the end of a very brief relationship. But he did take it, and for the moment he looked at her Jennifer was certain he was trying to think of some way to postpone saying good-bye.

He inquired, "Do you need a ride home or anything?"

Jennifer wished desperately she could have said yes. She admitted reluctantly, "I have to stay and help my sister count the receipts. I'll ride home with her."

He nodded, and once again the air was filled with things unsaid, promises unfulfilled, a lingering uncertainty and a reluctance to part. Or perhaps Jennifer had only imagined it, because his smile was impersonal and his voice casual as he slung the jacket over his shoulder and said, "Well, it was nice meeting you, Jennifer. Thanks for spending the evening with me."

And before she could even respond, he gave her a nonchalant wave, turned, and walked away.

Chapter Two

"Well, I think you were crazy to let him go," declared Jo Ellen, taking up the coffee tray and leading the way to the living room. "He sounds like a real doll—mysterious, too. Like something right out of your own crystal ball!"

"Jo Ellen Pierce," reprimanded her husband. "I can't believe you're actually encouraging your sister to pick up strangers at a fair! Besides, he wasn't all that good-looking—seemed perfectly ordinary to me. As for being mysterious," he pointed out wisely, "the only people who are mysterious are those with something to hide. You know, the criminal type."

"He wasn't a criminal," protested Jennifer, but Jo Ellen's voice overrode hers.

"For goodness sake, Phil," she exclaimed, setting the tray on the coffee table before the fireplace. "Stop being such an old stick-in-the-mud. You know perfectly well Jenny isn't the type of girl who 'picks up' men at fairs or anywhere else, but when someone interesting comes along, I say go for it. I mean, where else is she going to find anybody worth looking at twice? Certainly not in this"—she paused disdainfully over the word—*"village!"*

"You found me here," pointed out Phillip.

"That was twelve years ago," returned Jo, and Jennifer sighed, wishing she had never brought it up. Not that she had had any choice—naturally Phillip had informed Jo Ellen of the strange man Jennifer had "gone off with" last night, and what information Jo could not pry out of her on the way home yesterday evening she had succeeded in obtaining over dinner this afternoon. It was only natural, Jennifer supposed. Jo Ellen had been surrogate mother to her most of her life, and Phillip had stepped quite naturally into a paternal role when their father had died six years ago. Jennifer knew she should be grateful for their concern, but in fact it was a little annoying. Everyone thought little Jennifer needed taking care of, but little Jennifer had passed her twenty-first birthday five years ago and was far from needing taking care of—by her sister, her brother-in-law, or anyone else.

"What she needs to do," Phillip was insisting, "is marry that minister, what's-his-name?"

"Joseph Underwood?" exclaimed Jo Ellen, pouring the coffee. "She hasn't even been out with him."

"Adam asked me to fly to Paris with him in his Lear jet," said Jennifer mildly.

"Well, he'd ask her if she would just show a little interest," retaliated Phil. "It's plain to see he's interested in *her*."

"Jennifer, a minister's wife?"

"And when I said no, he took me in his arms and smothered me with mad, passionate kisses," continued Jenny, sotto voce.

"There are worse things," persisted Phil.

"Oh, don't be silly. Those people have to go wherever the church sends them, and Jenny wouldn't want to leave home."

"And then he threw me to the ground and ripped off all my clothes," concluded Jennifer, and her sister frowned at her mildly.

"Jenny, what a thing to say," she reproved.

"Do you see what I mean?" declared Phillip mildly. "She needs a steadying hand."

Jennifer sighed. "Look, the dinner was delicious, but if you two don't stop talking about me in the third person, I'm going to leave without dessert. I *don't* need anyone to manage my life for me, thank you very much—"

"Coconut pie," added her sister persuasively, and Jennifer hesitated for only a moment. Jo Ellen made the best coconut pie in two counties, and it was a hard invitation to refuse.

"We're not trying to manage your life for you, Jen," apologized Phillip as Jennifer dropped down beside the crackling fire and accepted the pie and coffee her sister offered. "We just worry about you, that's all."

"We care," specified Jo Ellen, settling down beside her husband with her own pie.

"Then will you please stop trying to marry me off to the minister?"

"I still think you should give him a second

look," insisted Phillip, and Jo Ellen elbowed him hard in the ribs.

Jennifer finished her pie and coffee quickly, then stood, announcing, "I'm going over to the library to finish cataloging that new shipment of books. Thanks for dinner."

Phillip stirred reluctantly. "I'll drive you over."

"Don't be silly." Jennifer pulled on her raincoat and scarf. "It's only a couple of blocks, and it's not raining that hard."

Phillip was obviously relieved. He was accustomed to an afternoon nap following Sunday dinner. "All right, then give me a call when you get ready to go home."

Although it wasn't raining much, the icy wind was vicious, and Jennifer walked quickly with her head down and her hands in her pockets, determined to take Phillip up on his offer of a ride home. She did not relish a muddy trek along the half-mile path that led to her house, and she suspected they might get a full-blown storm out of this drizzle before the day was over.

The small public library was dark and chilly, yet it exuded the familiar smells and muffled silence that meant home to her. This had been her sanctuary since she was a child; it was only natural that she should grow up to make it a permanent part of her life. The scent of dusty volumes, yellowing pages, and weathered hardwood floors enveloped her as she turned on the fluorescent lights directly over her desk, and the atmosphere settled quietly about her, barely disturbed by her entrance. She did not waste the township's money by turning on the furnace, but hugged her coat to her and rubbed her hands together to warm them as she settled behind the desk. She had truly intended to work this afternoon, but she found herself having to drag her thoughts away from the enigmatic man she had met last night and the few hours they had spent together. She kept seeing his face, the soft gray eyes, the troubled lines that seemed so out of place, the smile. She wondered where he was now, what he was doing. She wondered at her own gullibility, that she would allow herself to become so captivated by a man about whom she knew nothing, a man destined to disappear from her life as abruptly as he had entered. But then, that was the pattern of her life . . . happiness eluding her by inches, opportunities slipping by while she resigned herself to a fate of uneventful spinsterhood, even beginning to like it that way.

With a sigh she gave up on the boring chore of card cataloging and admitted she was in no mood to work today. The wind and the rain had increased in ferocity, flinging itself remorselessly at the high side window, and Jennifer abandoned whatever fleeting thought she had had about walking back to her sister's house. She would give Phillip an hour or two for his nap and then have him drive her home. She reached for a book and settled back, within moments forgetting all about Phillip and Adam Wilson and the growing storm outside, completely immersed in the newest national best seller.

It could not have been too much later that the front door opened on a blast of wind that scattered dead leaves and raindrops over the rubber mat and chilled her bare knees. She looked up, thinking Phillip must have become worried about the weather and decided to come for her early, but somehow the footsteps that approached at an easy, measured gait did not sound like Phillip's. And then a voice spoke out of the dimness, artificially sinister and uncannily familiar. "So, the local witch is in actuality the town librarian, passing her days poring over ancient volumes and her nights performing secret incantations.... This is beginning to sound like the plot of a low-budget TV movie." Adam Wilson stepped into the light.

The book slipped out of her hands and clattered onto the desk. "Wh-what are you doing here?" she said with a gasp.

He moved toward her with an innate, loose-limbed grace, his footfalls creaking on the hardwood floor. He was wearing only the jacket he had loaned her last night, his thick hair was rain-streaked, and his face looked cold and pinched, but if he was feeling the weather's discomfort, it did not show in his demeanor as he leaned casually on the desk and answered her. "I was at the crossroads of opportunity and took a wrong turn." At her stifled laugh he insisted, "No, it's true. I've been driving around in circles all night, and finally found myself back here. I think you put a spell on me."

"Now, why would I do that?" she demanded, the corners of her mouth dimpling.

"Perhaps," he suggested with a twinkle, "because you had an overpowering craving for my body?"

She swallowed nervously and crossed her arms over her thin chest, but she refused to drop her eyes. As she held his gaze something flickered within his eyes—surprise, at first, and then something more elemental that made her senses quicken in instinctual response. But then he dropped his eyes to the desk, and the moment was gone.

"Good book," he commented. "How do you like it?"

"It's enthralling," she answered, on comfortable ground now. "It's beautifully written and compelling—I couldn't put it down."

Once again there was a hint of unsettling, provocative laughter in his eyes. "You're not shocked? Scandalized? Outraged? What kind of small-town librarian are you?"

She frowned a little uncertainly. "I'm only on page fourteen," she admitted. "Should I be scandalized?"

He lowered his voice confidentially as he leaned toward her. *"The Tale of Elias Cotton,"* he told her, "has enough sex and violence in it to make Harold Robbins look like an amateur. The love scenes could be used as a marriage manual. Not to mention the incest, rape, murder, and explicit perversion that precede Elias's discovery of his own latent homosexuality—"

"Don't tell me the ending!" she protested, and he laughed.

"You're right, though," he said. "It's beautifully written, a moving story that somehow manages to be both poetic and ruthless—and compelling to the last page. It's destined to be a literary classic."

"Your opinion, or the critics?"

"Both," he answered, and they shared a smile.

"You sound like a man who loves books," she said, warming to this discovery. "Not one who simply enjoys them, but who really loves them."

"I'm a man who reveres beauty wherever he finds it," he answered her, and a momentary shadow flickered across his face. "And I admire people, like this author, who can create it out of even the most sordid reality." But then he looked up, and the momentary disturbance that had clouded his face was gone. "But I didn't come here to participate in a literary discussion panel."

"Why did you come here?" she interrupted him. "How did you know I worked here? The library isn't even open on Sundays."

"Intuition?" he teased her, and then admitted, "I saw you come in from the coffee shop across the street. I stopped by your brother-in-law's office first, but of course there was no one there. And before you get any ideas about being pursued by a ruthless playboy, let me hasten to explain that I sought out your brother-in-law purely for business purposes."

"Oh?" She hid her disappointment with a puzzled frown. She rather liked the idea of being pursued by a ruthless playboy . . . especially if the playboy was him. That admission surprised her.

"I was hoping he could put me in touch with

some short-term rental property around here," he explained.

"Oh." The excited pleasure that flooded her was totally inappropriate. "So you've decided to stay awhile after all."

He shrugged. "Why fight fate? I could use some peace and quiet, and this seems like as good a place as any."

She looked at him thoughtfully, once again struck by the lines of fatigue and stress on his face. His eyes were slightly bloodshot and mauve-shadowed, and she wondered if he really had driven all night. He certainly looked like a man in need of recuperative relaxation, as she had decided on first impression of him yesterday. She said in a moment, "I think I have an idea. How much are you willing to spend?"

"How much is it going to cost?" was the very urbane reply.

"How short term did you have in mind?"

"By the week would be nice."

She picked up the telephone and dialed Phillip's number.

He was not pleased to be awakened, but he grew more amenable when he realized money was involved. After a few moments' conversation Jennifer covered the receiver and spoke to Adam. "He says a month's rental is the best he can do, but he'll let you have off-season rates." And at a prompting from the other end, she added, "In advance."

Adam's lips tightened with a cynical smile, and after a moment he nodded. "Do I get to see the place first?"

"Oh, sure." She spoke to Phillip. "No, that's okay, I'll take him out and use my key. That way you won't have to get out in the rain. Right, I'll let you know."

"We'd better leave now," she told Adam as she slid off the stool, "if you want to get a look at the place in the daylight. The electricity isn't on. Do you mind if we take your car? I don't drive."

"Of course. But I didn't mean to put you to any trouble."

"No trouble," she assured him brightly, and then glanced at him. "As a matter of fact, you'll actually be doing me a favor—driving me home."

He paused with his hand on the door, his arm circling her, and the unsettling light in his eyes made her feel as though that stance were deliberate. "Why, Miss Kiel," he said softly, "are you suggesting that we may soon be sharing a mutual residence?"

"Not at all," she said quickly, and opened the door herself. It was ridiculous to let his teasing disturb her so. What had happened to her sense of humor? If only he wouldn't look at her so... sexily. "It's just that your place—that is, the place I'm going to show you—is next door to mine." The icy wind and rain cut off her chatter, and she was almost grateful for that as they ran toward the shelter of the truck at the curb.

Bear greeted her enthusiastically, and by the time it was possible to resume conversation, Jennifer was laughing and relaxed. Adam had started the engine and was waiting for directions. She gave Bear a casual command to sit, and Adam shook his head wonderingly as the dog settled down in the back. "That still amazes me," he murmured. "Do you work your magic on men as well as animals?"

She wisely ignored the question and instructed him, "Take this road straight out of town. It's a lake cottage," she explained. "My father built half a dozen of them and rented them out during the summer. They're all empty now, so you could really take your pick, but the one next to mine is the nicest. The rest of them need a little work before next season."

"You live there all year around?" he inquired.

"Um-hmm. Jo and I own them jointly now, but we leave all the details to Phil. He usually manages to keep them filled during the season, but I like it best when the tourists go home."

"Don't you get lonely?"

She laughed. "It's not exactly Lake Meade, you know. Just a small resort a few miles outside of town. Take the next left."

"How do you get back and forth to work," he asked as they started down the narrow, deserted road that led to the lake, "if you don't drive?"

"I walk. There's a little trail behind my house that leads to town. I think it used to be an old road. It's not that far from my doorstep to the library. Slow down," she advised, "there's a little turnoff here, and you'll miss it if you're not careful."

He had already slowed to barely thirty miles an hour. The driving rain pounded in sheets against the windshield, making visibility almost zero. A sudden gust of wind rocked the firmly based vehicle, eliciting a whine of concern from the back seat passenger, but the driver did not seem to be alarmed. He carefully made the turn onto the narrow dirt road, and the side windows were immediately engulfed by angrily whipping dead branches; the front window was a sheet of blowing water.

He leaned forward for better visibility as the truck crept along at ten miles an hour. "Now I see why you don't drive," he commented. "Without four-wheel drive you'd be stuck out here on days like this."

"Oh, it's really not so bad."

There was an overhead sound, a cracking or a splitting; he swore sharply and veered left, and Jennifer felt a hollow explosion of fear burst outward, and then . . .

"Jennifer!"

His hand was gripping her arm tightly, but she hardly felt it. His face was like a floating white moon before her eyes, his voice far away. Heavy weights pulled at her limbs, and she was swimming, swimming toward the convex bubble at the surface of reality. . . .

"Jennifer, are you all right? Are you hurt?"

She blinked once, slowly, and her surroundings fell painfully into focus: his face, white and strained; the roaring storm pounding on the roof of the vehicle; a warm panting in her ear coupled with anxious whines. Everything was just a little fuzzy about the edges, but the only thing she really felt was an awful sense of hollowness and fear in the pit of her stomach. . . .

"Jenny!" He shook her arm, snapping her head back, and she turned to look at him.

The grogginess was still enveloping her, but a sudden surge of adrenaline made it easier to combat. She thought there must have been an accident; that was why the truck was no longer moving, and perhaps he had not noticed. "What?" she snapped at him.

"Are you hurt?"

"No," she responded briefly, and pulled her arm away. Her heart was pounding hard, and it made her head hurt. *Please don't let him have noticed, don't let him ask. . . .*

He looked at her a moment longer, oddly, searching her face, and he insisted, "Are you sure?"

"I'm sure." Once again her voice was sharper than it should have been. She tried to bring it down to a normal tenor. The painful straining of her heart within her ribs did not make it any easier. "I'm just . . . shaken a little. Shocked. What about you?"

The strange, uncertain look disappeared gradually from his face. "A big tree—or part of one— crashed down in front of us," he explained. "I stopped before we hit it, but I think we went off the road. Hold on; let me go check the damage."

The door opened on a blast of wind and rain, and when he was gone, Jennifer fought the almost overpowering urge to sink back against the upholstery and give in to the weighted lethargy. This time fear was her ally—fear and concern for him kept her alert. Bear nuzzled her neck anxiously, and she reached back to ruffle his fur, smiling weakly. "It's all right, boy," she whispered. "Nothing to be scared of."

The few minutes Adam spent outside left him soaked from the skin outward. His hair was plastered darkly to his scalp, and he wiped rivulets of water from a face that was white and drawn with discomfort. The "waterproof" jacket hung wetly about his torso, and the jeans were molded to his thighs. He grimaced and made an unmistakable sound of pain when he reached to slam the door behind him.

Immediately all signs of lethargy left her as Jennifer cried, "You *are* hurt! What—"

"I just scratched my arm on something outside," he responded briefly, tight-lipped. "We're blocked from the front by the tree, and the back wheels are sunk in about two feet of mud. We're stuck." Then he looked at her grimly. "If you're such a damn great psychic, why didn't you predict *this*?"

Jennifer saw no alternative. "My house is just a couple of hundred yards up the road. You could see it if it weren't for the rain. We can walk."

He hesitated. "It's pretty rough out there. Maybe I should go and call someone."

She half laughed, feeling a surge of power at being in control of the situation. "That's the city boy in you talking. We New Englanders do for ourselves. Come on!" Her hand was on the door handle and she was clambering out into the storm before he could protest further.

The description "pretty rough" was mild indeed. The moment she stepped out she sank to the tops of her boots in icy mud. She had to hold on to Bear's collar to regain her balance, and the wind kept knocking her back. She couldn't see and she could hardly take a deep breath without choking on rain. By the time Adam had helped her to climb over the fallen tree, her hands and legs were so numb she did not even feel the scratches and bruises she suffered at her many falls. Adam put his arm about her waist, but after the first few hundred feet it seemed as though she were supporting him, instead of the other way around. She plunged on blindly through the icy ocean, urging him to keep up, and her legs felt like icicles that threatened to shatter with each step.

Jennifer almost stumbled over her own threshold, and she gasped out loud with relief as her numb fingers closed over the key. She was shaking so badly it took forever to get the key in the lock. Adam leaned against the door frame beside her and did not offer to help.

Even the moderately warm interior felt like a furnace compared to the frozen storm they had just left. Bear squeezed in beside her, and Adam followed more slowly. She hit the light switch with the palm of one hand and turned the thermostat up full blast with the other. Her fingers were numb, but her feet and legs were beginning to tingle unbearably. She stripped off her soaked coat and let it drop to the floor, immediately grabbing up an afghan from the sofa and wrapping herself in it. She could hear the sounds of Adam's strenuous breathing above her own gasping and chattering, and in a moment he pushed himself away from the door with a concentrated effort and began to pile logs into the fireplace.

A small yellow-blue flame was licking at the logs by the time she had regained enough control of her voice to speak. "I'm—going to get out of these—wet clothes. You should too. You—" And then she stopped, coming over to him in swift alarm. "Your arm!"

"It's okay," he said briefly, but it obviously wasn't. Blood was trickling over his fingers to mix with the water that dripped from his jacket in a bright pink stream. She could tell by the long rip in the sleeve of the jacket that the injury was more than just a scratch.

"Good Lord," she said in soft alarm, kneeling beside him. "What did you cut it on?"

"I don't know." His voice was tight, possibly with an effort to control his shivering. "The cold seems to have slowed down the bleeding. Maybe you should give me something to wrap it in."

She was racked by another violent shiver, which the warmth of the glowing fire could do little to mitigate. She left him for a moment and returned with a towel, her teeth still chattering. "I'll—change, and then—bandage it for you. T-take off your wet things and I'll put them in the dryer. There's a—blanket in the chest over there."

The effort of that broken speech completely exhausted her, and she did not wait for a reply. She hurried to the bedroom to change.

Her clothes were not so much wet as they were simply cold—unlike Adam, who had not had the protection of an all-weather coat. Her feet throbbed when she pulled off the frozen boots, and she spent a long time rubbing circulation back into them. The activity warmed her, and by the time she pulled on a flannel robe and tucked her feet into fur-lined slippers, her teeth had stopped chattering. She hurried to the bathroom for the first-aid kit and then back to the living room.

The floor-length brushed-flannel robe she wore was of a lavender-wallpaper print, high-waisted, and trimmed with baby lace at the gathered sleeves and modest neckline. She had never considered it a particularly fetching garment, and the surprised light of recognition in Adam's eyes startled her. She had also given no thought to the fact that the buttons ended at the knees and she had worn nothing underneath it. She was suddenly self-conscious about the length of bare leg that was exposed when she walked, which was silly. She quickly hid her embarrassment by scolding Adam. "You're still wearing those wet clothes! You're going to get pneumonia!"

He was sitting on the hearth feeding the fire to a roaring blaze that danced in beautiful shadows across her golden hardwood floor and picked up the lustrous highlights of her simple pine furniture. For just a moment she could imagine the circumstances were different and the sight of his lean masculine form gracing her hearth sent the very faintest shiver of warm excitement and pleasure through her, but that reaction was very faint and very far away, totally inappropriate. Because of course there was nothing romantic about his presence here at all; he was wet and frozen and his face was white and pinched with discomfort, the dark smudges about his eyes even more pronounced than they had been before. He had wiped most of the moisture from his face and hair and removed his jacket, but his hair was still dark with rain and his sodden sweater clung to him like a second skin. The hem of his jeans dripped water onto the stone hearth, forming puddles there. Jennifer felt faintly annoyed with him as she sat beside him and unwrapped the towel from his arm.

What she saw there caused a momentary sickness to go through her. Jennifer had not had much experience with injuries or illness, and she did not handle the sight of blood very well. It was a moment before she could control her distaste and say, rather weakly, "I think . . . you're going to need stitches."

"I doubt that." His voice was curt, and he took the first-aid kit from her, attending to his own wound with one hand while she watched helplessly and felt foolish. It was true that the cold had slowed the flow of blood, but that only gave her a better view of the ugly long gash on his forearm, a ragged tear that seared the white flesh with angry red. The thought of the pain he must be feeling made her feel sick again.

He applied antiseptic and wrapped the arm rather clumsily with gauze, trying not to wince as he did it. Her own weakness and helplessness made Jennifer angry, and she took it out on him. "You're a real macho type, aren't you?" she accused somewhat breathlessly. "Sitting around in wet clothes freezing to death—why didn't you change like I told you?"

"Into what?" he returned shortly, not looking at her as he taped off the bandage.

"Don't tell me you're shy!" she gibed on a bark of laughter brought on purely by stress.

He looked at her calmly, his eyes as clear as glass and just as hard. And he said in a smooth undertone that made her very uneasy, "No more shy than you are, little small-town librarian."

Jennifer did not know how to take that. She felt a sudden danger in the way he looked at her, a palpable tightening of the atmosphere between them, and she did not understand that, either. She only knew that she had no right to bark at him, and she regretted her acerbic tone. She said more persuasively, "Look, this is silly. You can undress in the bathroom and wrap yourself in a blanket; your clothes will be dry in half an hour. We're both adults here, after all—"

"Yes, aren't we?" Adam's voice was very soft, and the way he looked at her made her retreat into sudden confusion. It was not an amorous look, exactly, but the sexual undertones were unmistakable. It made Jennifer suddenly aware of the flimsiness of the garment that had always seemed very substantial before and of her nakedness underneath. It made her feel threatened.

She swallowed hard, not knowing what to say, and as she gazed back something flickered uncertainly in his eyes; he looked abruptly toward the fire. His next words were so curt and unexpected that she thought she must have misread the look that had gone before, and she was both alarmed and embarrassed. "No need," he said briefly. "I'll just get wet again when I go back outside."

"Go back—!" Amazement cut off her words. "But—where will you go? Why would you want to go back out in that storm?"

He turned back to her slowly, his voice even and his expression enigmatic. "You did say there was another house here? That is why we came?"

"Yes, but—" she floundered, and spread her hands helplessly. "You can't go there now! Look how dark it is; you couldn't see anything now, even if it weren't for the storm." She shook her head on a breath of exasperation and got to her feet. "This is about the stupidest conversation I've ever had. You just get undressed and get dried off and I'll make us something to eat."

She started to turn toward the kitchen, but he got slowly to his feet beside her, blocking her way. She tried to tell herself that the hardness in his eyes was only from discomfort and the grim lines at his mouth merely a sign of pain and fatigue, but the change in him went deeper than that. He no longer seemed to be the man she had met last night at the fair, nor even the one who had come so casually into the library this afternoon. There was a wariness about him, something basic and animalistic that might have been generated from tightly controlled anger far beneath the surface.

Even Bear sensed it and registered the fact in a sudden pricking of his ears as he got cautiously to his feet and stood close to his master. Jennifer was completely disoriented and even more confused by the smoothness of the words that followed.

"Very nice," he said softly. His eyes seemed to go right through her and did not particularly like what they saw. "A cozy meal sitting naked by the fire, warm and secluded and completely alone, listening to the storm, going to bed...."

She couldn't believe he meant what the words implied. It was totally inappropriate under the circumstances, and somehow seemed out of character for him. "O-of course," she stammered, trying to maintain a realistic grasp upon the truth of the situation, "you'll stay here tonight.... I mean, I suppose you have to. You can't go back to town and the—the house next door doesn't have any electricity or—or dry firewood; you'll freeze. I can make up the sofa."

"Sure you can." His finger came out to touch her jaw; it traced a light, cold path along the curve of her face and down her throat to her collarbone, over the line of bare chest at the closing of her robe. Jennifer's heart raced even as she shrank back, her eyes searching his face in both anxiety and alarm. She couldn't believe he was serious; she couldn't believe he had taken a perfectly innocent situation and twisted it around so...The hard gleam in his eyes both confused and frightened her, because it seemed to hold a tinge of disgust. "Nice try, lady, but I'm too tired and wet and cold to take you up on it tonight," he said flatly, dropping his hand. "You're a cute kid, but give me a break this time, will you?"

She gasped audibly and took an indignant, totally incredulous step backward. "What," she demanded in a voice made tight with outrage and disbelief, "are you suggesting?"

He gave a short, bitter laugh, and his eyes snapped with something that bore only the very faintest resemblance to amusement. "All right, you can drop the scandalized librarian routine— although I've got to admit it almost worked there for a minute. You and your wide gold eyes and your maternal concern and that sweet little night-gown—nice touch. But, to put it bluntly, I'm not that hard up for a woman, and if I were, I wouldn't have come back here. So if you'll just—"

She couldn't believe this. Pure anger slashed through the incredulity his sudden transformation had produced, and she cried furiously, "Why you—how dare you! How *dare* you suggest that I—"

"Enough with the phony innocence!" he shot back. "I tell you, I'm just too damn tired for the game tonight. You've been coming on to me since I first met you yesterday afternoon, with your pretty blushes and your simpering remarks, and to tell you the truth, you almost had me convinced. But you sure picked a hell of a time to get serious about it."

"I suppose you think I arranged the storm just to—to seduce you!"

He regarded her coolly, and the chill went

straight to her bones. "No," he answered easily, raking her up and down with his eyes. "But you sure didn't waste any time taking advantage of it, did you?"

Her face was burning and she was shaking; she could not recall ever having been quite so angry—or so disillusioned—with anyone in her life. She curled her fists into tight balls against her thighs, and all she wanted to do at that moment was to hit him. "You son of a—"

"Nice language, Pollyanna," he interrupted, and there was a faint satisfaction in his eyes that belied his totally expressionless tone. "Now, if you'll just give me the key—assuming there actually is one—and point me in the direction of the alleged house...."

She couldn't face him any longer. If she did, she was certain to do something violent. She would not let him do this to her. Her hands were shaking as she fumbled through the drawer for the set of keys, struggling for control. She would not let him upset her to the point of... *What nerve! What an incredible ego!* He wasn't worth the fury she was feeling now; he wasn't worth the humiliation or the outrage.... She found the set of keys and jerked at the proper one until the rubber band that held them together broke and spilled keys all over the floor with a clatter. She rescued the correct one and whirled on him, holding it out to him stiffly. She was proud of the evenness in her voice as she demanded, "Will you just tell me one thing? How did you ever get such an inflated opinion of yourself? What makes you think that every woman you meet has nothing on her mind but getting into bed with you?''

"Experience," he replied briefly without the slightest pretense of shame. "So why don't you just drop the moral outrage," he continued mildly, "and admit that the only reason you're mad is because I turned you down? Didn't you just say a minute ago we're both adults? And we both know the score. So kindly stop looking at me as though your next move is likely to be homicidal and be civilized enough to at least offer me a flashlight.''

He was serious. She couldn't believe it, but he was really serious. Totally convinced of his own desirability and her promiscuity, he was handling the entire situation as though it were a scenario he had acted out many times before. The sophisticated urbanity of it made Jennifer's stomach churn.

She turned blindly back to the desk and pulled out a flashlight, slapping it into his outstretched hand without a word. Sardonic amusement flickered in his cold gray eyes as he said simply, "Thank you." He turned to pick up his wet jacket and inquired, "Which house?''

"Try them all until you find one that fits the key," she snapped, and the quirk of his eyebrow made her want to hit him again. He pulled on the dripping jacket and came back over to her. "One other thing," he said smoothly. "I take it on the run. I don't get hooked up with small-town girls who forget to take their pills and have a bevy of male relatives with loaded shotguns—''

Then she did hit him. Or at least she tried. He

caught her hand at the wrist just before it made contact with his face and lowered it with very little force back to her side. In that moment, as he looked at her heaving chest and glittering eyes, something flickered across his face—it might have been regret, or perhaps it was simply astonishment at her unexpected display of violence. But then he released her wrist and said lowly, "Hell. I knew this was a mistake." He made a soft sound to summon Bear, and turned toward the door.

"I hope you freeze!" Jennifer shouted after him, but the door opened on a blast of cold wind and rain, and he was gone.

Chapter Three

The morning brought a crystal stillness of the sort only the aftermath of a storm can produce. The sky was a brilliant autumnal blue, and the trees stood stark and barren witness to the ravages of the landscape below. The lake was a motionless sheet of glass around which clumps of colorful leaves floated like broken ornaments. Scattered branches, flattened bushes, and two uprooted saplings bore mute evidence of last night's devastation, and as Jennifer turned away from the window she found herself wondering absently what Mr. Adam Wilson intended to do about the fallen tree blocking the road. It could stay there and rot as far as she was concerned.

It would have been nice to comfort herself with the fact that she had lost no sleep over her new neighbor's—if that was what he was—erratic behavior, but unfortunately that was not true. She had lost a great deal of sleep fuming over him, worrying about him alone in that dark empty house—if he had even made it that far—wondering what had made him turn into a monster, and fretting over the possibility that at least some of his accusations might be true.

Hadn't she only yesterday admitted to her sister that she found him attractive? Hadn't there been times the night before at the fair when she had wanted to be kissed by a perfect stranger? *Had* she made suggestive remarks to him, or had something shown in her eyes she had not been aware of? And if he had stayed last night, if circumstances had been different and he had stayed...? But that was ridiculous. She was not the type of woman who went to bed with a man just because she was asked, certainly not with a perfect stranger, and she most emphatically would never do the asking herself.... The gall of him! The more sleep she lost, the more furious she became, and by the time the obscenely brilliant sun broke through her headachey grogginess, she would have been happy never to have heard the name of Adam Wilson again.

Jennifer listened to the morning news reports of the storm that had blown out to sea while she made coffee and dressed for work, and then she informed the meteorologist with biting ill humor that hindsight was better than no sight at all. Her disposition only worsened as she thought more about the events of the night before, and as she pulled on galoshes for the muddy trek to town she was looking forward to a hard walk to work off her anger.

But her temperament softened as she opened the back door and found a large black Newfoundland waiting patiently on her step. "Well, hello."

She smiled and reached down to pet him. His fur was dry, which at least told her he had spent the night indoors. Presumably Mr. Self-Confidence had found the house to which the key fit, though how he had kept warm during the night she did not know and didn't care. "What is this, a social call, or are you looking for some breakfast?" She glanced up self-consciously, half-expecting the shadow of the animal's master to fall over them, but he was nowhere in sight. She wondered what *he* had done for breakfast.

She straightened up, now confident that the dog had come alone, and looked toward the house a few hundred yards down the winding lane. Nestled in the shelter of deciduous trees that had forfeited all but their most tenacious leaves, it was perfectly visible this morning. It was still and silent; no smoke curled from the chimney and no sounds carried across the lake to hint at human occupancy. Perhaps he hadn't stayed there after all. Maybe he had gone back to the truck or even hiked into town.... Then she scowled in irritation with herself and dismissed the worry. It was no concern of hers what he had done.

She gave the dog a final affectionate slap on the shoulder and told him, "I've got to go to work now, boy. You stay here...or find your master, or do whatever you're supposed to be doing."

Bear whined as she turned away and lifted his paw, very much as though he were extending the apology his master had not the decency to make. Jenny could not help smiling as she took the furry paw, and then she knelt to give the animal a swift hug. When she left, he stood there and looked after her for a time, but made no attempt to follow. When Jennifer looked back just before the trail to town curved to obscure the lake, the dog was making his way at a sedate pace back toward the house next door.

Phillip walked over to the library at noon and invited her to lunch. "Thanks for the business, by the way," he said, and grinned over his tuna sandwich at the local café. "Does this mean you get to keep my commission?"

For a moment she was confused, and then she said, "Oh, you mean he's decided to stay?" That did surprise her, for more reasons than one.

Phillip nodded cheerfully. "He was in bright and early this morning with a month's rent in advance—in cash. I understand you had quite an adventure last night."

Jennifer picked off the crust of her sandwich, her appetite rapidly diminishing. "There was nothing adventurous about it," she muttered. "Just a fallen tree and a good drenching. How did he get his truck out?"

Phillip shrugged. "He must have been up at the crack of dawn. The truck was a mess; looked like it had fallen in the lake. Did he really stay in that place last night without any electricity?"

"I guess."

"He said something about buying a chain saw to get that tree out of the way; he might be able to get some dry firewood out of that. I told him I wouldn't be able to get the utilities turned on until tomorrow, but he seemed determined to stay there tonight. Not that he had much choice," admitted Phil prosaically, "unless he wants to drive twenty miles for a motel. Funny, too, he didn't strike me as the rugged outdoor type. Looks like he'd be more comfortable in a posh hotel suite with room service and one of those Jacuzzi bathtubs than out chopping wood for a place that doesn't even have running water yet, you know what I mean? He had on a pair of jeans this morning with that fancy designer stitching on them, and what kind of man carries around that much cash, I'd like to know...."

Jennifer was wondering how he was going to chop firewood—or operate a chain saw, for that matter—with an injured arm. But that, too, was none of her business. She told Phil pleasantly, "You have the mentality of a small-town gossip, you know that, Phil? It's a habit you really should try to curb."

Phillip feigned insult, but he was not really offended. He knew Jennifer too well to take any of her barbs seriously...which was rather a shame, Jennifer thought absently.

When she got home that evening there was still no sign of life from the house next door. Curiosity prompted her to walk down the road in the failing light, and she discovered that the tree had been reduced to rounded chunks and branches and removed to the side of the road. Obviously it was too wet to be used as firewood. Midway back to her own house the large black dog met her, and as she greeted him absently she noticed that the blue Blazer was parked on the other side of the house next door, so that it had been obscured from her view when she had first come in. So he was going to spend another night in that house without heat or light; and temperatures were predicted to drop near freezing.... It only went to prove what she had been thinking all day. He was an idiot.

Bear politely walked her to the door and prepared to leave her there, but she impulsively invited him in to partake of the three quarters of a meat loaf left over from Friday night's dinner. As she watched the dog wolf down what was, to him, a mere snack, she wondered absently what his master was doing for dinner. She had planned to make herself some soup, and the neighborly thing to do... But no. Let him eat out. Of course, she could walk over and invite him to help himself to her firewood.... But she had no intention of doing anything so foolish. Let *him* make the first move. She wasn't even sure she would accept an apology from him now if he offered one, and as for food or firewood or anything else.... She turned firmly away from the window.

Bear was licking his chops and looking at her expectantly, but when she apologized and spread her hands helplessly he did not seem too disappointed. He offered her his paw again, and she laughed as she took it, telling him, "Too bad your master couldn't have acquired some of your manners!"

She spent the evening trying not to worry about the man next door in the cold dark house who hadn't had any dinner.

Jennifer saw Adam the next morning as she was leaving for work. He was trying to split green firewood on a stump at the side of the house and was not doing a very good job of it, either. Jennifer considered that a matter of too little too late, since the electricity would be turned on today, but apparently two nights in a freezing house had convinced him any action, even a foolish one, was better than none. She noticed that his movements were stiff and labored, and she thought his arm must be paining him a great deal. For a moment she was moved to pity, and she started to call out to him, but pride stopped her at the last minute. She had had all the humiliation she could take at the hands of this man, and he had made it abundantly clear he wanted nothing from *her*. She walked away without speaking, and he did not look up.

Joseph Underwood came by the library, presumably to borrow some books, but even Jennifer was not so naive, or so near-sighted, not to realize the real reason for his visit was simply his desire to talk to her. He was a pleasant young man, and she always enjoyed their visits, but today he made the mistake of bringing up her new neighbor.

"His name is Adam Wilson; he's a photographer from Chicago on his way to Canada; he's thirty-six years old, and has a big Newfoundland dog named Bear," responded Jennifer, somewhat testily, "and that's all I know."

The young minister lifted an eyebrow mildly. "A mite touchy on the subject of Mr. Wilson, aren't we?"

Jennifer frowned and busied herself with stamping the due date on the books he had selected. "I just get a little tired of the way gossip travels around this town. You'd think he had come here in a spaceship or something."

"Well, you've got to admit, Jennifer, we don't get many strangers through this time of year, and anyone who would rent a lake cottage with the first snow only weeks away is bound to be considered a little strange—present company excluded, of course." And then he smiled most charmingly. "Besides, my interest is purely professional. He might be a prospective parishioner, after all."

Jennifer gave a short, mirthless laugh as she presented his books to him. "I doubt that!"

"May I drive you home?" he asked unexpectedly.

Jennifer hesitated for only a moment. She could not help remembering Phillip's opinion of the minister's interest in her, and she found that somewhat disturbing. But on the other hand... She smiled at him teasingly. "Planning to buttonhole the new resident?"

He took her coat from the rack. "That," he assured her, "was the furthest thought from my mind."

Jennifer took her purse and her own selection of books for the evening, and he placed his hand lightly upon her back as he walked her to his car.

Jennifer liked Joseph Underwood; their conversation was always easy and witty; and he was not afraid to argue with her. She looked forward to his biweekly visits to the library and was always glad of a chance encounter upon the street or at a community social affair, but she had never considered him more than a friendly acquaintance.

She was therefore quite taken aback when, as he stopped the car in front of her house, he paused in what seemed like a moment of awkwardness before saying good night. And when he spoke, he did not say good night at all, rather a somewhat halting, "Jennifer, I'd like to ask you something before you go inside—if you don't mind."

Jennifer had been watching the house across the way, noticing with something like relief that the windows glowed with electric light. The blue truck was parked just where it had been this morning. She wondered what he had done all day. Joseph's words brought her eyes to him with a pleasant smile, and she was surprised to notice what might very well have been a faint blush on his face in the uncertain light. But even that did not prepare her for what he was about to say.

"Jennifer," he began, and hesitated. Then he plunged on, "Jennifer, I'd like to see you—socially, I mean. We've known each other for some time now and . . . well, I know you're not seeing anyone else and I wondered . . . if we might have dinner together some night. Just the two of us."

Jennifer had not received such an awkward invitation since she was a teenager, yet she was moved by the sentiment that had prompted it. She realized suddenly that arranging a social life must be uncomfortable business indeed for a man in his position, for he was under the constant scrutiny of his congregation, the church elders, and the members of the community. In the eighteen months he had been here he had not been seen with any woman other than in a purely ministerial capacity; she knew the decision to ask her out had not been made lightly. And that was what made her uneasy.

Her hands tightened upon the books in her lap, and she found she suddenly could not meet his eyes. "Joseph," she began carefully, "please don't think I don't appreciate the invitation, or— or that I'm not flattered.... " She felt him tense beside her, and she rushed on, anxious not to hurt him. "But..." She looked at him. "Do you think it's wise? You know how the people in this town talk, and a man in your position... What I mean to say is, for us to be seen together in public would...imply a commitment, wouldn't it?"

He relaxed. His eyes held hers steadily. "I'm not averse to a commitment," he said quietly.

But Jennifer was. At least under these circumstances. Joseph was nice, he was pleasant-looking, and they got along well together, and had he been anyone other than who he was, she would not have thought twice about accepting a date with him. In fact, he was practically the only eligible male in her age group in the entire town, and she should have expected this sooner or later. It would be very easy to fall into a quiet courting relationship with him, eventually into marriage.... And that's where she balked. With any other man it would have been the easiest thing in the world, but when the minister of a small-town Methodist church asked a young woman to go out with him the clock was suddenly turned back two centuries and it was tantamount to a marriage proposal. Their names would be linked together like chain mail from the first date onward, and there were only two possible resolutions to the relationship: marriage or scandal. He knew that as well as she did, and that was why the careful deliberation with which the invitation had been issued frightened her.

He smiled tolerantly, although somewhat uneasily, as he understood her silent reservations. "I know it's complicated," he said gently. "That's why I never asked you before...though I wanted to. I never took a vow of celibacy, Jennifer," he told her. "I expect to marry—in fact, I should have done so before now, but it would take a very special type of woman to accept the partnership I could offer her...." And then he smiled and shook his head a little. "I'm not doing a very good job of this, am I? I wish it could be simpler."

Jennifer did not know what to say. What *did* one say when an invitation for a first date and a marriage proposal came hand-in-hand?

She looked at him helplessly, and he read the answer in her eyes. He dropped his own eyes, however, before she could see what registered there, and when at last he spoke, the words were, once again, unexpected. "May I ask you again?" he inquired.

She looked at that soft, gentle, somewhat shy face, and she felt a brief surge of anger for the small-town mores and conventions that placed them in such an awkward position. She fumbled with the doorknob, stammering, "I—I'm not sure, Joseph. I don't think—"

He smiled as she got out. "I'll ask you again," he decided. "Good night, Jennifer."

Jennifer tried not to be troubled by the episode as she went inside and began heating up the leftover soup for her dinner. It was really stupid: She liked Joseph, and he liked her; why couldn't they enjoy each other's company in a noncommittal social relationship without the fear of being stigmatized or pressured into a commitment? Because Jennifer knew without a doubt she would never want to marry him. She enjoyed his company and valued his friendship, but there simply was no excitement there, no chemistry, no...attraction. Not, for example, as there had been with...But she determinedly pushed that thought aside as she sat down at the table with the warm bowl of soup and a glass of milk. She wished briefly that she had the courage to flout convention and ignore public opinion and go out with Joseph just for the fun of it, but she knew she did not. And neither did he.

She sighed as she absently stirred the soup in her bowl, and she found her thoughts wandering once again to the man next door. Perhaps it was the absence of the dog that had made her think of him tonight. She realized that she had grown used to Bear greeting her in the morning and meeting her when she came home at night, and she wondered if perhaps his master had gotten wind of the arrangement and kept him locked up. He certainly did have a lot of lights on over there, she noticed as her gaze wandered unbidden to the kitchen window. It was as though he were making up for the two nights he had spent in darkness by turning on every light in the house tonight. He had a fire going, too. It must have finally occurred to him that he could buy firewood easier than he could chop it himself. She felt another flicker of irritation with him and the entire situation. What had ever made him decide to stay here? And were they really going to be neighbors for the next month without a word passing between them? They were the only two people on the lake, and it would be only decent of him to make some sort of effort toward a civilized relationship. Especially since everything had started out so well between them. She remembered again the man she had met at the fair and she couldn't believe that she had misjudged him so, that he had transformed so radically....

Now the irritation was directed at herself as she forcefully put him from her mind and picked up a book. *She* had done nothing wrong, and it was up to him to mend fences. She was crazy to give him a second thought.

Within moments she was completely immersed in *The Tale of Elias Cotton,* and she did not think about the peculiar behavior of the man next door again all evening.

At one thirty Jennifer turned the last page, her eyes misted over with the beauty of the story of one man's passage into manhood, the courage and dignity with which he had learned to face life and accept himself. It was exactly the sort of courage Jennifer had been looking for all her life, and it sometimes seemed that just when she started to close her fingers about it, it slipped through her grasp without a trace.

She put the book away and went to bed pleasantly weary, nostalgically sad. When she turned off the light she could not help noticing that every light in the house next door still blazed.

It seemed she had barely closed her eyes when she was awakened by an awful racket. Sounds were magnified by the stillness of the lake and whatever was banging and scraping against her door sounded as though it would take the entire house down. She switched on the light and squinted at the clock. Three A.M. She groaned and buried her head in the pillow, thinking something groggily about a loose branch or perhaps an overturned trashcan. But the noise did not cease, and now it was punctuated by a series of distinct, urgent barks.

She was alert, sitting up in bed and listening. Bear. What could be wrong with him this time of night? Was he lost? Hurt? Or just making a nuisance of himself?

Whatever, she obviously was not going to get any sleep until she took care of him. With a groan she pulled on her robe and slippers and made her way sleepily to the back door.

As soon as she opened it the big dog pushed inside, almost knocking her to the floor as he flung his full weight against her legs and deafened her with a sharp, anxious bark. She caught herself against the counter and exclaimed, "What in the world is wrong with you? Do you have any idea what time it is? What—"

But Bear had no time for the amenities. With another bark deep in his throat he dashed outside, stopped a few feet away, and ran back to her anxiously. He repeated the charade once more, and Jennifer realized incredulously that the dog was trying to get her to follow him. She had too great a rapport with animals to ignore this most basic communication, and she knew such behavior was not generally prompted by whim. Her heart began to thud in swift alarm as she realized something must be wrong at the house next door. A fire? An accident?

Impatiently Bear caught the sleeve of her robe and began to tug, and Jennifer assured him quickly, "All right, I'm coming. Let me get my coat."

She flung her coat over her shoulders and followed the dog outdoors, and immediately her fears about a fire were allayed. Everything seemed to be perfectly normal next door, despite the fact that all the lights still shone brightly enough to light the path without the help of the moon. She was beginning to feel rather foolish, and when the large dog wiggled through a recently installed pet door, Jennifer hesitated, afraid to knock. What if, despite the dog's alarming behavior, everything was perfectly all right inside? His master would hardly appreciate being awakened at three o'clock in the morning. . . . But he couldn't be asleep. All the lights were on. A terrible dread began to knot in her chest, and there was no use arguing with her instincts; she *knew* something was wrong.

Jennifer tried the door, and it opened without hesitation. Bear was waiting for her impatiently in the kitchen, and she called out somewhat timidly, "Adam?"

Only Bear's anxious whine replied, and the echoing silence seemed somehow sinister.

She called again, more loudly, "Adam!"

Bear barked sharply and ran toward the hallway that led to the single bedroom. Jennifer followed more slowly, dread and fear mounting with each step.

The bedroom light was bright and merciless, confirming more or less her worst expectations. Adam was upon the bed, the bedclothes twisted around one bare leg and tossed away from his torso. His hair was damp and tangled limply over his forehead, his terrifyingly white face marred only by dark ghoulish smudges beneath his eyes and two bright streaks of scarlet that ran from each temple to his cheeks. His breathing was labored and uneven, sounding almost choked, and Jennifer felt a fear like none she had ever known as she listened to the sound of his breathing. She made herself cross the room.

Through a haze of helplessness and dread she noticed that the bandaged arm was red and puffy above the white gauze; when she touched his forehead tentatively, his skin seared her fingers. Desperately she tried to think; she tried to calm the racing of her pulse and the roaring in her ears that obscured the choked sounds for breath he was making. He was ill, perhaps dangerously so, and what was she to do? Jennifer had no experience with such things; she had never had to take care of anyone before. Everyone always took care of Jennifer; everyone was always so careful not to upset Jennifer.... But now Jennifer was alone with a crisis on her hands, and she had to deal with it.

Suddenly he opened his eyes. But before relief could register, the dread only increased. His eyes were glassy and unfocused and startlingly bright; he looked at her for a long time, and she was certain he did not recognize her. Bear whined anxiously at her heels, prompting her into speech. "Adam?" she said softly. When he made no response, she leaned closer and spoke more firmly. "Adam, it's Jennifer."

The twitch of his lips might have been an effort to smile. His voice was barely a croak. "Why—am I surprised?" he said.

"I—I think you're sick," she said, and then bit her lip with the inanity of the statement. *Do.* She had to think of something to *do.*

"I think so too," he whispered, and closed his eyes wearily. "I'm so ... thirsty."

"I'll get you some water." She could do that. *Damn,* why did this have to happen to her? Why not Jo, who was always so competent and calm, who knew how to deal with everything, who was never afraid....

She left the room quickly and started for the kitchen, but once there she stopped, took one calming breath, and determined to take hold of herself. She could deal with this. She was the only one here, and she had to. It was obvious he was very ill, but it was unlikely that he would die, and she could surely take a few minutes to think what was the best thing to do. There was no need to panic.

Jennifer decided she could at least take his temperature and proceed from there. She made her way to the large, old-fashioned bathroom and switched on the light, and for a moment was disoriented. The light bulb had been replaced with a red one, and the muted glow it gave off was eerie, casting familiar fixtures into unfamiliar shadows and spotlighting the addition of pieces of new equipment. It took her a moment to realize he had transformed the bathroom into partial use as a darkroom, but then she ignored the photographs that were hanging from the ceiling and tacked to the walls and made her way to the medicine chest. She found a thermometer and a bottle of aspirin after much fumbling through bottles of photographic chemicals, closed the door behind her, and hurried back to the bedroom.

He was awake again, and this time seemed almost lucid. "God, I feel so stupid," he groaned. "What are you doing here, anyway?"

"It doesn't matter." She shook down the thermometer. "You have a fever. Can you hold this under your tongue?"

He winced as though feeling a sudden pain and turned his head. "I was going to return your flashlight," he said hoarsely. "I should have done it before. I thought you would be mad. I don't blame you."

"Adam, please." She touched his burning cheek. "I have to take your temperature."

He looked at her. His eyes were filled with suffering and burning with fever; she felt a tightening in her stomach in empathetic response to him.

"I acted like an idiot," he said. "I wanted to tell you that...." And then his brows tightened slowly, as though in great concentration. "I think I'm delirious. You shouldn't listen to anything I say. You shouldn't be here."

"I know," she said soothingly, as though to a child. "I won't. Just let me put this in your mouth."

"I'll do it." He took the thermometer from her. "Can I have something to drink?"

"After we get your temperature. Can you ... ?"

He put the thermometer in his mouth and closed his eyes.

Jennifer went to get him a glass of water, and when she returned she blanched at the reading of the thermometer. Now she was really frightened. At what temperature had she read that brain damage could result? How long had he been like this? With shaking hands she placed the thermometer on the bedside table and helped him to sit up to drink the water. The heat of his bare shoulders penetrated through her coat and her robe and reminded her of a bad case of sunburn.

He drained the glass and then lay back weakly against the support of her arm, breathing heavily. She thought quickly. The county hospital was twenty miles away, but she did not think that was the wisest course. Even if exposure to the night air did not endanger his condition more, she had serious doubts about her ability to get him to the car. "Adam," she said as calmly as she could, "your temperature is over a hundred and four and you need a doctor. Do you have a telephone yet?"

"No," he muttered, not opening his eyes. "People call when you have a telephone."

She eased her arm away from the heavy weight of his shoulders, pushing the pillows up to support his head. Even the pillows were hot. "All right," she said. "Adam, listen." He opened his heavy-lidded eyes, and crystal gray sparks glittered at her. "I'm going next door to phone a doctor. I'm sure he'll come out. You'll be all right here for a few minutes. Don't try to get up. I'll be right back."

And suddenly he smiled at her, beautifully and brilliantly. "What do I need a doctor for, witch? You can lay your hands on me and cure me in an instant."

She could not help returning the childlike smile that accompanied the nonsensical statement, and she smoothed his tangled hair away from his forehead. "I'm afraid healing is not among my psychic powers," she told him, and started to rise.

His eyes suddenly clouded, and he gripped her hand with hot, dry fingers that were amazingly strong. "No. Wait. Don't go." Urgency lined his face, and the clasp of his hand was painful.

"I'll be right back," she assured him.

"But..." The word trailed off into a fitful mumble. "It doesn't matter...." And he turned his head. She had to pry his fingers away from hers.

It took the doctor forty-five minutes to dress and drive out. That was the longest three quarters of an hour Jennifer had ever spent. She stayed with Adam, alternately pacing the floor and sponging his face with cool cloths while he tossed and moaned fitfully in his sleep. Bear settled at the foot of the bed, apparently convinced everything was under control, but he was the only one in the room who was calm. Over and over Jennifer berated herself. She was the one who had let him go out into the storm and spend two days in this house without heat. She had known how badly injured his arm was, and she hadn't insisted he seek medical attention. Two days had passed, and she had deliberately avoided offering him firewood or even a hot meal. . . . She had practically wished this on him!

When the knock on the door came, she ran to it, a growling and barking Bear at her heels. The dog stood at the door, hackles raised and teeth bared, ready to lunge at the intruder. Jennifer told him sharply, "Stop it!" and did not hesitate about opening the door. When Dr. Thompson came in, the dog watched him warily but did not attack.

"I wouldn't do this for anyone but you, Jenny," the middle-aged man told her cheerfully. "Where's our patient?"

Gratefully Jennifer led him to the bedroom.

When the doctor returned almost half an hour later, his face was sober. "It's a systemic infection caused by that gash on his arm," he told her. "His resistance must have been pretty low. How long has he been like this, do you know?"

Jennifer told him about the injury two days ago, about his exposure to the storm and the nights spent in the cold house, and that she had seen him chopping firewood only this morning, even though he had seemed to be in a great deal of pain. The doctor nodded thoughtfully. "Sounds as though he was trying to get sick, doesn't it? Well," he added with a smile as he closed his bag and turned to her, "while I won't say you exactly saved his life, I am glad you called when you did. How did you happen to be over here, anyway?"

He must have realized the tactlessness of the question, even as she realized she was still dressed in her nightgown and robe. Only the presence of her coat lent authenticity to her story about the dog, and she still wasn't sure he believed her. Not that it mattered. Dr. Thompson was one person—perhaps the only person—in this town who could be relied upon to be discreet.

He said, "I've drained the arm and given him some stitches and a massive dose of antibiotics. I'd say the prognosis is good, but..." He hesitated. "Does he live alone? He's going to need some careful attention the next few days, and he might be better off in a hospital."

Jennifer swallowed hard. "Is it—really that serious?"

"Ordinarily no," admitted the doctor, "especially considering the shortage of hospital beds. But he certainly won't be able to do much for himself for a while, and we can't just leave him here alone."

"I'll stay," Jennifer found herself volunteering. She owed him that much.

The doctor looked hesitant, but all he said was, "And how are *you* doing?"

"I'm fine," she assured him. "I've never felt better."

"I'd like to have a report every now and then," he reminded her, and then he smiled, gripping her shoulder bracingly. "I'm proud of you, Jenny," he said gently, and Jennifer felt her courage swell. She was proud of herself too.

He gave her several bottles of medication with instructions on how often they should be given and promised to return tomorrow. When Jennifer returned to Adam, he was sleeping, not peacefully by any means, but at least sleeping. His face was still starkly white and drawn with pain; he tossed his head restlessly and mumbled incoherently in his sleep. The antibiotics had not yet taken effect, and his skin still burned her fingers when she moved to draw the blanket over his chest. He immediately pushed it away, groaning out loud at the pain caused by the abrupt movement of his freshly bandaged arm and, of course, completely careless of his nudity. Jennifer covered him again, waited until he was still, and then silently turned off the light and went to put the medicine bottles in the bathroom.

This time she stopped to notice the photographs. She couldn't help it, because the first one she saw was of herself. It had been taken at the fair, the "sexy" pose she had struck for him with her head thrown back and her hair pushed up.... She felt a tingle of something close to embarrassment mixed with the nostalgia of the memory. The other photographs he had taken that night were there too, all of the same face from different angles, arrested laughter and frozen words captured against the blur of color in the background.... He was very good. There were other pictures, landscapes and scenery mostly, old buildings and picturesque bridges, and then, to her amazement, she discovered another set of photographs of herself. Only these... She took one down and examined it in the eerie light, frowning. These had been taken here, at the lake. There was one of her kneeling at the back door, hugging Bear, another of her walking down the trail with the afternoon sun forming a golden halo around her head, another one of her simply standing outside her cottage, gazing thoughtfully directly into the lens of the camera. She cast an uneasy glance over her shoulder. When had he taken these? And why? And...

A sudden hoarse, piercing cry shattered the stillness of the house and burst through her reflections, whirling her around in galvanized terror. As she ran down the hallway it came again—punctuated this time by Bear's alarmed barking—the agonized, heart-stopping sound of a man's scream.

She burst into the room, tripping over Bear and bumping into the nightstand as she fumbled for the lamp, her heart racing and thundering so abandonedly that it shook her entire body. She found the switch and stumbled onto the bed, reaching automatically for arms that flailed with animallike strength and threatened to knock her to the floor, crying, "Adam! It's all right—stop it! You're going to hurt your arm! Stop!"

He was sitting up in bed, his eyes wild, gasping for breath as his mindless struggles ceased. He was drenched with sweat as the fever still burned, and he gasped, "I couldn't see! Why couldn't I see? It was dark—"

"It's all right," she whispered breathlessly, her heart thumping in a painful rhythm against her ribs as she tried gently to push him back against the pillows. "I turned off the light. It's night, that's all. You're all right."

His fingers closed around her wrist with a painful grasp and his eyes were glazed and incoherent. "Bad dream," he muttered. His eyes were already beginning to droop closed. "Couldn't remember ... where I was."

"I know," she soothed. "It's all right now."

"Don't like ... the dark," he managed with a great effort. "They sneak up on you ... in the dark."

Jennifer's frown was puzzled and tender; she stroked his brow as she would that of a child in similar circumstances, and gradually the strained look of terror and pain relaxed from his face. Exhausted, he lay back against the pillows and closed his eyes. He was breathing hard, and he still held her wrist in a firm grasp. When she tried to pull away, the fingers tightened and he whispered hoarsely, "Stay. Please stay."

And so she sat beside him throughout the night, guardian against the bad dreams, waking him at intervals to administer his medication and to offer him water, and she kept the light burning.

Chapter Four

By eight thirty Wednesday morning the fever seemed to have eased somewhat, and Adam was sleeping for the first time almost naturally. Jennifer felt it was safe to leave him long enough to go home and change her clothes and to call Jo and ask her to have someone open the library for her. Jo Ellen found the situation very interesting, but Jennifer minimized it as much as possible, telling her sister that she was just being neighborly and no, there was no reason for her to drive out.

The long night had taken its toll on Jennifer. Her head ached and her eyes were scratchy, and she included the makings of a strong pot of coffee in the grocery bag she filled with juices and soups to take next door. She did not take time to unpack the bag when she arrived, however, but went immediately to check on her patient.

He was sitting on the side of the bed wearing a blue kimono robe, his head resting in his hands and looking as though he might pass out any moment. Jennifer exclaimed, "What in the world are you doing?"

"I just went to the bathroom," he muttered.

She came quickly over to him. "By yourself?"

He looked at her; she was overwhelmingly relieved to see that his eyes were clear and lucid, though badly bloodshot and still marred by dark shadows. "It might surprise you to know," he returned dryly, "that I've been doing exactly that since I was two years old."

She tried not to laugh from sheer joy that he was himself once again. "Do you need any help?" she offered.

"Thank you." Now the sarcasm in his tone was obscured by weariness. "I managed the trip there and back just fine—with a little help from my friend." He made a movement as though to stroke the dog at his feet, but apparently that effort was too much for him. His hand trembled as he straightened up.

Now he looked at her as if for the first time comprehending her presence, and something close to horror mingled with the incredulity in his eyes. "Jesus," he said softly. "You really were here last night...." And his voice trailed off into weakness. His face tightened with the effort to ease himself back onto the bed and slowly lie down; he was breathing hard when his head rested against the pillows. Jennifer was poised to help, but she did not touch him until he was settled.

She pulled the blanket over his bare feet and legs and explained, "Bear came to get me. Lucky for you he did, too; you were pretty sick."

A very faint smile traced his white lips, and he murmured without opening his eyes, "Funny thing about animals. They don't rationalize; they just *see*. They see things we don't sometimes. I guess that's why he's always liked you so much."

Jennifer hesitated, afraid that he might be slipping into delirium again, and then she said gently, "It's time for you to take your pills. I'll be right back."

He took the pills without protest and lay back down again, obviously exhausted. Jennifer thought he would sleep, but as she turned to leave he spoke unexpectedly. "Must have been a hell of a night for you," he said wearily. He opened his eyes slowly, and his expression was slightly anxious. "I've been told I'm not a very good patient."

"Oh, you weren't so bad," she smiled. It was good to hear Adam talking rationally again, even though she knew he probably shouldn't be wasting his strength. "You scared me a couple of times, though."

His eyes suddenly sharpened. "What did I do? Did I say something?"

"No," she assured him quickly. "You were just delirious, that's all. Adam..." She could not prevent the frown of concern from registering on her face. "Your fever was dangerously high. I was—I was afraid it might be more serious than it was."

He closed his eyes and replied briefly, "I'm surprised you cared."

She caught her breath for an angry retort, but he interrupted her. "Wasn't the doctor here?"

She hesitated for just a moment, but she could not really be angry with him. Self-pity was a notorious trait among sick people, and he should not be held responsible for that last remark. Calmly and gently she told him what the doctor had said.

"Hell." He sighed bitterly. "And I thought I'd had a change of luck. What a stupid thing to happen." He gave her a look that was too sharp and too biting to be teasing and challenged, "Didn't the famous Madame Voltaire herself tell me just last week that things were looking up?"

"Well," she responded shortly, finding it hard to be patient with him, "it seems to me you brought a great deal of your present difficulties on yourself. You're a grown man; you knew that arm needed medical attention. Any fool knows how to prevent an infection. And as for your noble display of braving the elements and spending two nights in an unheated house... do you have a death wish or something?"

He closed his eyes and turned his face away from her. He said very quietly, "Maybe I do." Then, in the wake of her stunned silence, he brought a hand shakily up to push back his hair and said tiredly, "Ah, hell. Don't listen to me. I told you I'm a bad patient. Just go away, will you?"

Jennifer left, closing the door quietly behind her.

Jennifer tried to convince him to take some soup for lunch, but he was not interested. He accepted the juice she offered, however, and when she tapped out the prescribed pills into his hand he looked at them skeptically before demanding,

"Which one of these is making me sleep so much?"

"They're all antibiotics," she told him, "except the yellow ones. They're for pain."

He scowled and tossed the yellow pill away. Glaring at him, Jennifer retrieved it and deposited it in the trash. "Another display of macho heroism?" she challenged him sarcastically, but he looked away.

"I just don't like dope," was all he would respond.

And just as she was turning to go he said with a note of weary apology in his voice, "Look, I hate this. I hate being sick, and I'm furious with myself for letting it happen. To tell you the truth, I'm not real crazy about having you take care of me, either, so why don't you just do us both a favor and forget the Florence Nightingale act? Go home."

Jennifer faced him calmly. "No," she said. A faint scowl of irritation creased his drained face, but she forestalled his further objections by responding firmly, "I'm staying until the doctor says you can take care of yourself."

"Why?" he insisted uncharitably. "You certainly don't owe me anything."

"Maybe I do," responded Jennifer, and a light note of teasing underscored the mock thoughtfulness of her tone. "After all," she reminded him with a lift of the eyebrow just before she flounced out of the room, "it was my spell that brought you back here, wasn't it?"

The doctor's late-afternoon visit was encourag-

ing only to the extent that no new complications
had developed. He told Jennifer that Adam appeared to be out of danger and that he should find
his strength returning in a couple of days; meanwhile he was to be watched carefully and was not
to over-exert himself.

Adam's fever rose again after sundown, but
Jennifer was not alarmed. The doctor had told her
to expect that. The truculent, uncooperative patient of the afternoon was now only a very weak,
very miserable man, and Jennifer was glad she
had not let him talk her into leaving. She sponged
off his face and forced him to take fluid and aspirin as the doctor had instructed, and she sat beside
him as he tossed and mumbled incoherently in a
tortured sleep. Toward midnight he began to calm
down somewhat, sleeping more quietly and for
longer periods of time, and Jennifer thought it
was safe to leave him. She gave him his last dos-
age of medication and told him she planned to
make up the couch for herself and that if he
needed her he was to call.

Adam made no comment, but when she reached
to turn off the lamp, he said with a quick urgency
that reminded her all too well of the night before,
"Don't do that."

She looked at him questioningly, but he only
closed his eyes and turned his face away from her.
"Just don't," he repeated in a calmer tone, and
he looked and sounded exhausted. "Please."

It was exhaustion that finally forced Jennifer
into a restless sleep, but she lay awake a long time
on the uncomfortable couch, thinking about the

man in the next room and trying not to wonder why the torment he was undergoing now seemed to be so much more than physical.

The next morning he looked worse, if possible, than ever. While he was still sleeping Jennifer had gone home to shower and change, and when she returned he was once again sitting up in bed. His hair was dull and tangled; his face looked washed out and was covered with a bristly stubble of blond beard. His cheeks were hollow, and the sunken dark pockets beneath his eyes made his face look like a papier mâché mask. "I feel terrible," he greeted her, scowling.

"You look like the feature attaction in a horror show," she retorted.

And then, to her very great surprise, he smiled, weakly and ruefully. "You're a real glutton for punishment, aren't you?"

"Am I?" responded Jennifer thoughtfully. "What makes you think so?"

The effort it had taken for him to smile showed in the defeated, rather sullen lines into which his face fell now. "Don't tell me I've overestimated my capacity for nastiness," he said. "I would have thought that after two days of this you would be ready to run for cover and think twice about volunteering yourself for any other charitable duties."

"I never thought of myself as a charitable person," Jennifer admitted, "but if that's what you want to call it, that's all right with me. And as for your capacity for nastiness—I'm not intimidated.

I'm a pretty bad patient myself. There's nothing worse than being helpless and sick and dependent on other people—unless it's having people fussing over you when you're not sick.''

Jennifer received the impression that that statement, which was meant to be no more than prosaically understanding, was somehow exactly the wrong thing to say. His face suddenly tightened, and a hardness came over his eyes, which were no longer focused on her. And he said simply, "Yes." He looked back at her, reserved and distant. "So you know how distasteful it is to be dependent on others, and you won't be offended when I tell you that I'd like to postpone that eventuality as long as possible. Will you please go home now?"

"No," responded Jennifer cheerfully. "But I'm going to work for a few hours as soon as I fix your breakfast. Will you eat some hot cereal if I make it?"

"No," he said darkly. "I'm going to get out of bed now and take a shower. You can either hand me my robe or prepare to be embarrassed."

"It's a little bit late for modesty, I'm afraid," replied Jennifer as she brought him his robe from the chair on the other side of the room. "You weren't particularly concerned with it the first night I came here, and if I were going to be shocked, it would have been then."

Once again Jennifer was reminded that he was a man who generally found it easier to smile than to scowl, even in his present condition of misery. There was a lightening of the strained lines on his face, and his tone almost could have been teasing as he lifted an eyebrow. "You weren't?"

"I only could have been shocked," she pointed out, "if I had seen something unusual. Believe me, you're very usual. Nothing shocking about your body at all."

And with that parting comment, which she thought might in some small way begin to pay him back for the insults he had delivered to her the other night, she left. She would have been gratified to see the slow, rather weak grin that spread over his face in response.

While he was in the bathroom she made the bed with fresh linen and then returned to the kitchen to make breakfast. Jennifer knew that it probably was not a good idea for him to be up, but she also knew there was very little she could have done to stop him. So she simply waited anxiously until she heard him return from the bathroom, then gave him a few minutes to get settled before she brought the tray.

He was sprawled out on top of the freshly made bed, still wearing his robe and looking exhausted. The grayish tint to his face told her that the exercise had not done him much good, but he tried to disguise from her his labored breathing and trembling muscles. The nicks upon his face were the evidence of his attempt to shave, but he explained to her ruefully as she paused at the door, "It looks as though the shower will have to wait." He tried to sit up, and winced sharply as he inadvertently put pressure on the injured arm. *"Damn,"* he said tightly, "I hate this." He scowled as she set the tray on the table beside him. "I told you I didn't want anything to eat."

"You might change your mind later," she replied patiently. "I'll be back to fix your lunch. Do you need anything before I leave?"

He simply looked at her, and slowly his expression changed into one of weary resignation mixed with incredulity. "You really don't know when to give up, do you?"

"I'll be back," she assured him.

Jennifer had qualified assistants—one full-time and one part-time after school—and she was not really worried about the one day she had missed from work. Still, there was a lot to catch up on, and it took longer than she expected. The twenty minutes spent on the telephone explaining to Jo what the situation was with her new neighbor did not help Jennifer's schedule any. It was almost one thirty before she began the walk back home for lunch.

She used her key to let herself in the back door, and was surprised to find Adam up, dressed in jeans and an unbuttoned wool shirt, standing in front of the open refrigerator door. He turned when she came in. "Where the hell have you been?" he demanded.

Jennifer set her purse and the books she had been carrying on the counter and returned, "What are you doing out of bed?"

He took a bottle of juice out of the refrigerator and closed the door. "I was hungry," he replied, and Jennifer could not help smiling at the almost childlike note of accusation in his tone. He recognized it too, and in a moment acknowledged the fact with a rather sheepish expression.

He poured a glass of juice while Jennifer hung up her coat, and then she said, "Get back into bed. You look like death warmed over. I'll fix you some soup."

He slowly and deliberately recapped the orange juice, not looking at her. "Do you remember what you said this morning about having people fussing over you? I don't like it either. I'd really rather take care of myself."

"And did it ever occur to you," responded Jennifer evenly, "that if you don't follow the doctor's instructions now you may have people 'fussing over' you for a lot longer than just a couple of days?" She took the bottle from him and replaced it in the refrigerator. "If you think this is bad, just imagine how you'd feel in a hospital."

"I don't have to imagine," he returned briefly, "I've been there, and I don't like it one bit." He drank from the glass, leaning against the counter, and watched her steadily. Then he said, "Why are you doing this?"

Jennifer took a pot from the cupboard and set it on a burner. The answer surprised even herself. "Because sometimes it feels good to do something for someone else." She had never thought about that before. Perhaps because she had never had an opportunity to do anything for anyone before, not in any meaningful way. The feeling of being needed—even by so reluctant a beneficiary as he—was an alien one to her.

She opened a can of soup and poured it into the pot. "Are you feeling any better, or is this all just another tough-guy act?"

"I feel like hell," he informed her bluntly. "My arm feels like it's been through a Cuisinart and my head is throbbing and every muscle in my body aches. Satisfied?"

"Are those little yellow pills starting to look any better to you?"

He lifted one shoulder in a disgruntled shrug and made his way carefully over to the table, where he sat down slowly, trying not to show what an effort that had cost him. "I told you before, I don't like dope," he answered. "I saw too many good people wasted because of it in Nam," he added with a surprising attempt at communicativeness. She gave him a surprised, questioning look, but he only shrugged. "It's a waste of time to go around half bombed, anyway." He focused his eyes on the clear autumnal view from the kitchen window, contemplating the crystal blues of the sky and the lake, the dashes of orange and brown that clung to the skeletal black and gray trees, the feathering of white in the wild shrubs that grew along the lakeshore. "You miss so much," he added thoughtfully, almost to himself.

Jennifer knew only too well the sentiment he expressed, and for a moment she felt the same easy harmony they had shared the night of the fair. There was a sad, almost haunted look on his face as he gazed out the window, and Jennifer wanted to question it, to encourage him to speak his thoughts out loud...to share with her whatever it was that was torturing him so. But then he looked away from the window, sipped again from his glass, and the moment was gone.

He noticed the books she had left on the counter. "What's that?"

"I thought you might like something to read while you were convalescing," she replied. "I wasn't sure exactly what your tastes were, so I brought a little of everything—romance, suspense, science fiction, even some nonfiction, in case you're feeling intellectual."

Adam looked at her for a moment; then he dropped his eyes. "That was nice," he said quietly. "Thank you." And when he looked at her again there was a look of impatience in his eyes—directed at himself, not at her. The lines about his mouth tightened, and he said curtly, "All right, I kept hoping if I ignored it it would go away, but it hasn't—and it's obvious you're not going to go away—so I guess I may as well get it over with. I owe you an apology for the other night. Will you accept?"

Jennifer stirred the soup, took a bowl from the cabinet and a spoon from the drawer, then turned to face him, leaning her palms on the counter and regarding him calmly. "No," she said simply.

A look of surprise and, perhaps, just the faintest trace of defeat registered on his face before she went on reasonably, "But I might be interested in listening to an explanation."

He glanced down at the half-empty glass of juice, a small smile playing at the corners of his colorless lips. "How about a couple of excuses?

Like I was tired and wet and cold and in a great deal of pain? Like I have a rotten temper, and I don't always do a very good job of controlling it? Like I had a lot on my mind. . . ."

She shook her head silently, and he shrugged, wincing a little at the movement of the injured arm. "All right," he said in a moment on the breath of a sigh. His eyes wandered restlessly to the window again and focused there. He spoke without looking at her. "Obviously I misread the whole situation—and the worst part is that I think I did it on purpose." Now he ventured a brief glance at her, then looked quickly away. "I guess you could say I have a rather jaded attitude toward members of the opposite sex. I had no right to take my disillusionment out on you. Especially," he admitted, "since you gave me no reason to do so."

Jennifer was silent for a moment, but then she could no longer ignore the curiosity that had been bothering her since their first meeting. "This . . . jaded attitude of yours," she ventured, "does it have something to do with your marriage?"

He made a short sound that could have been a mirthless laugh. "Just because my ex-wife would sleep with anything in pants? No, that couldn't be it." And then he looked at her sharply. "How did you know . . . ?" He broke off into a dry smile. "I forgot," he answered his own question. "You're a witch."

"How long have you been divorced?" she asked.

"Almost a year," was the brief reply. He finished the orange juice and looked at her. "So, am I forgiven, or did you let me go through all of that just so you could have the satisfaction of throwing that soup in my face?"

She turned and poured the soup carefully into the bowl. "I haven't decided yet. So far I've gotten a lot of excuses and no good explanation."

"Bottom line, huh?" He looked at her frankly, no sign of uneasiness or evasion in his face now whatsoever. He told her, "Maybe I was just trying to scare you off. There's no room in my life right now for involvements."

Incredulously Jennifer realized he was doing it again. "Involvements!" she exclaimed. "Who said anything about involvements? All I did was do my brother-in-law a favor and bring you out here to show you the house—at *your* request, I might add! I never did or said anything to give you the impression that I was interested in any sort of—involvement!" That is, she had to admit rather uncomfortably to herself, unless he could read her mind...which perhaps he had been doing since the moment they met. She had been attracted to him, that she could not deny, and perhaps she had done something that he had read as a come-on...or perhaps he simply thought that any woman under sixty was fair game. The entire situation annoyed her, mostly because he had done his best to nip the relationship in the bud before she had even had a chance to make up her mind whether or not she wanted to see it blossom.

She set his soup before him with a disgruntled, "Eat it before it gets cold." But he surprised her by touching her wrist when she started to move away. His fingers were warm—not feverish, but pleasantly warm, and soft. He let his fingers fall away when she looked at him, but the memory of his touch remained. And the look in his eyes startled her. It was gentle, strangely assessing; it made her pulses speed without her knowing why and a warmth start somewhere in the region of her chest and spread slowly outward.

He said quietly, "It's hard not to get involved with you, Jennifer. You've haunted me since the first moment our hands touched and sparks flew.... You drew me back here when I didn't want to come, and everything that's happened since then has only been designed to make me more involved with you." He took a short breath and looked away from her briefly. When he went on, the tightness was back on his face, the distance creeping back into his eyes. "It was nothing personal," he said, and the obvious non sequitur apparently referred to his behavior on the night of the storm. "It was just that I came here to get away from it all, to find a quiet place just to be alone and sort out a few things, and I didn't plan on . . . having to deal with other people. I just don't have time. . . . I met you at a very bad time. Under other circumstances . . ." He trailed off.

Jennifer could make no sense of this at all. The look in his eyes when he had talked about being involved with her had precipitated a feeling of quick excitement within her, a rush of warm anticipation, but his concluding statement had all but negated what had gone before. In one way, however, it did explain his sudden change of attitude toward her since the night of the fair. He had enjoyed her company only for as long as he thought he would never see her again, but when it became obvious they would be neighbors, he construed their acquaintance as a threat to his privacy. Then... "Why did you stay?" she asked curiously. "Why did you come back at all?"

He smiled, weakly and rather ruefully. "I think we'd better close that subject for the time being. I've talked too much already, and I'm going to get into trouble if I'm not careful. Besides, I don't imagine I'm making too much sense. My head is spinning, and my stomach feels like a lump of Jell-O." He looked distastefully at the soup before him. "Do I have to eat this?"

"Only if you want to get your strength back," replied Jennifer. "But you've probably been up too long. Why don't you go back to bed and I'll bring it to you there."

"No thanks," he replied dourly, and picked up his spoon reluctantly. "I've seen enough of that bedroom to last me awhile. I'd rather stay out here."

"All right then," she said, and started to turn. "I'll leave you alone."

He looked up quickly. "Do you have to go back to work right away?"

She hesitated. "No. But I thought you said..."

"Forget what I said. I'd like it," he added, almost shyly, "if you could stay and talk to me for a while. Old Bear is pretty good company, but he's not a great conversationalist, and besides, after the past two days you owe me a chance to prove to you I'm not really a raving maniac. In fact, I used to be a pretty nice guy; I guess I just haven't practiced the technique in so long I've forgotten how. What do you say? Give me a chance to be civilized for a change?"

After a moment she pulled out the chair beside him and sat down. "You're a very strange man, Adam Wilson," she said.

There was a hint of sadness to his brief, absent smile. "Not really. Just an ordinary guy caught up in some rather strange circumstances."

"Like what?" she prompted curiously.

But he declined to answer, turning his attention to the soup.

She decided to try a slightly more neutral approach. "Are you a free-lance photographer?" she inquired.

"Only in the sense that 'free-lance' means unemployed," he answered. "I used to work for one of the big Chicago dailies."

"What happened?"

The quirk of his brow was noncommittal. "A lot of things. Job burnout, I suppose. The last six months or so I've just been sort of traveling around the country, gathering shots for a friend of mine in New York who wants to put together a pictorial about the American way of life...as if there weren't enough of those already."

"You're very good," Jennifer said impulsively, and at his surprised look she felt a blush tingle. "I couldn't help noticing your darkroom," she admitted.

"Oh-oh." Now there was a spark of amusement in his clear gray eyes. "I've just left myself wide open for an invasion of privacy suit, haven't I? You saw the pictures I took of you—proving you're not a witch, by the way."

The blush only deepened, but she was glad he had brought it up. "As a matter of fact," she said, "I was wondering—"

"I used a telephoto lens," he told her. "And I was strictly ethical—I only photographed you when you were outside and in plain view and fully dressed."

"That's reassuring, I suppose," murmured Jennifer.

"Not, let me hasten to add," he assured her, "that I couldn't have invaded the sanctity of your home if I had wanted to—that lens is great for shower shots and bedroom peeking. I think I should be congratulated on my self-restraint."

Jennifer could not help laughing, mostly from sheer pleasure at the improvement in his mood. Once again he was the man she had met at the fair, and all that had passed between that time and this was no more than a minor puzzle to be examined in more detail later. "What kind of newspaper did you say you worked for in Chicago?" she teased him.

"A very respectable one, I assure you," he answered. "But before that I specialized in pin-up nudes for slick, high-priced magazines with worldwide publication." He watched her carefully for a reaction, and when she gave none he lifted an eyebrow. "Not shocked?"

"The only thing that shocks me," she responded thoughtfully, "is that you would want to waste good film and an expensive lens photographing me from across the lake." Her lips tightened with a repressed smile. "Fully dressed and in plain view out of doors. It sounds like a misuse of talent to me."

He smiled, and the unexpected softening in his eyes caught her off guard. "I try to capture beauty wherever I find it," he said. "And you..." He looked at her in a way that made her wonder what he was seeing. She could not imagine that there could ever be anything in her very ordinary face or gangly, straight-planed body to put that look in his eyes. "... are very beautiful."

In an effort to hide her confusion she made an awkward attempt to change the subject. "Is that your quest in life, then?" she returned lightly. "To seek out truth and beauty and preserve it on film for all posterity?"

There was a sardonic twist to his lips as he responded, "Imagine Dionysius with two left feet and a flashlight with a faulty battery, and that's me." He dropped his eyes, following the circular motions his spoon made in the bowl of soup, and she sensed the reserve creep back over him again, a tension that was the evidence of something he needed to say but did not want to share. "I was an AP photographer in Vietnam," he said at last, and the words were so swift and harsh they were almost blurted. "I don't guess I have to tell you what kind of material I had to work with there; you probably saw most of my pictures—the ones the censors didn't get to first.'' There was a dark bitterness to his words, a cold marbleizing of his face. ''I guess I saw all the ugliness, the filth, the lies, and the evil of the human race in those two years. . . .'' There was a brief silence, as though he were forcefully pushing back memories and confessions he dared not make. When he glanced at her again, there was a shadow of a smile on his face; the hardness in his eyes was being pushed into quiescence. He continued in a slightly easier tone, ''So when I got back to the States I took another course. I sought beauty and ended up photographing soft-core porn for an annual income that embarrasses me to think about. I sought truth, and I ended up doing plane crashes and fires and rapes and assassinations.'' He shrugged. ''Truth and beauty are just two more of those illusions in life that seem to disappear when you take a second look.''

She looked at him for a moment, wondering about him, wishing it were possible to reach out and comfort him, to do something to take that haunted, disillusioned look off his face . . . only beginning to understand the truth about what had put it there. She said quietly, ''Are you as bitter as you sound?''

He refused to meet her eyes for a moment. ''I hope not,'' he said softly. And then, looking at her honestly, he added, ''I try not to be.''

In that moment he had been so open and unrestrained with her that she did think she understood him, the idealistic young man who had been too soon exposed to the horrors of war and death, the visionary whose rose-colored glasses had been stripped forcefully from him.... He was a man who treasured beauty but had seen evil in its harshest colors, and the shock of that discovery had been printed indelibly on his mind. Jennifer felt something tug deeply within her heart toward him, a need, a compassion, a companionship.

Bear wiggled in through the pet door and went happily to greet first Jennifer, and then his master. The moment was gone. "I think I'm jealous," Adam said dryly. There was a glint in his eye, and it made her happy just to see him relax. "You never did tell me: Does your magic work on everyone, or only on overgrown puppies and bad-tempered thirty-six-year-old little boys?"

She dimpled. "You should see what I can do with an irate library committee or a short-budgeted school board."

"That's all right," he smiled, looking at her as he stroked the dog. "You've already made a believer out of me."

He placed his half-finished bowl of soup on the floor for Bear, and Jennifer pretended to be insulted. "Never let good food go to waste," he defended himself, unabashed. But when he straightened up, he swayed a little; Jennifer could see the swift draining of what little color was left in his face, and she took his arm quickly to steady him.

"All right," she said firmly. "That's enough. You're going back to bed and no arguments."

"Damn," he said quietly, angrily, and he gripped the edge of the table for support when she cautiously released his arm. "Do you have any idea how frustrating this is?"

"Yes," Jennifer answered calmly. "I do. It's no fun being sick, and it's even less fun having people watch you while you're sick, but trying to pretend you're as strong as an ox is not going to get you anything but sicker. Stand up slowly, now, because if you fall down I don't know how I'm ever going to get you up again."

A rather crooked grin played at his lips, disguising the short, shaky breath he took to steady himself. "I guess I could have worse nurses," he admitted. "I really am sorry I've been giving you such a rough time.... It was a matter of male pride as much as anything else, I think."

She stood beside him, lightly touching his shoulder to urge him to his feet. "We'll talk about that later," she told him firmly. "Get back to bed."

She followed his slow, weary gait to the bedroom door, where he paused and turned to her. The walk had made him short of breath, and a faint glaze of perspiration clung to his forehead, but he tried to ignore it as he requested casually, "Could I at least have something to read?"

She went back to the kitchen, and when she returned with a book he was lying upon the bed, leaning back against the pillows, breathing hard. Jennifer felt a stab of guilt for not having insisted he return to bed sooner; she worried about a relapse. She paused beside his bed, frowning with concern, and he opened his eyes when he sensed her presence. He smiled weakly. "Don't worry, I wouldn't have the bad taste to die in your presence." He held out his hand for the book, murmuring, "There's nothing worse than going to bed alone. Thanks for bringing a friend."

She released the book to him reluctantly. "You should really sleep."

"I will, eventually." He had already opened the book to the title page, and he read everything—copyright, publishing history, acknowledgments—with the same absorption he would a riveting passage of text. But when she turned to go, he looked up. "Will you be back today?"

She lifted an eyebrow mildly. "Do you want me to come back?"

His smile was rather sheepish. "If I answer that I might lose my reputation as a grouch. Yes," he said. "I want you to come back."

She tried to hide her pleasure with a nonchalant tone. "All right then, I will—on one condition."

He looked at her questioningly.

"That you tell me the real reason why you came back here," she said.

His hand marked his place in the book, and he looked at her for a long time thoughtfully. She knew he was debating whether or not he could tell her the truth—and if so, how much of the truth he should reveal. And when he spoke she knew that his answer, however enigmatic, was strictly candid, unembellished and unreserved. "I was looking for a miracle," he told her simply, "and this seemed like a good place to find one."

Jennifer turned away, puzzled, touched by something deep within him she could not define, wondering if she would ever really understand him . . . and wondering why it suddenly seemed so very important that she try.

Chapter Five

The library was open until noon on Saturdays, and Jennifer used the time to catch up on all she had missed because of the odd hours she had been keeping the past two days. As she walked home through the crisp autumn air she noticed that all was quiet at the house next door; not even Bear was out running around. When she had gone over yesterday evening to prepare Adam's dinner, he had been completely immersed in the second of the six books she had brought him, so much so that he had eaten the light meal absently and forgotten to complain about not being hungry, constantly casting his eyes toward the book he had put aside in a concession to good manners. He had picked it up again immediately when she took his tray away, and Jennifer thought he had not even noticed when she left. His light was still burning when Jennifer went to bed, and she knew how it was to be caught up in a book and to be unable to sleep until it was finished. She thought he had probably stayed up late last night reading and was sleeping late today; she did not hurry about going over there.

She did some light housework, made herself some lunch, and then followed the path between their two houses at a leisurely rate, enjoying the crystal blue day that was, indeed, larger than life. She let herself in quietly with her own key in case he might still be sleeping and greeted Bear in a whisper when he came wagging his tail to meet her. But when she looked up, she was surprised.

The kitchen opened onto the living room, and she could see Adam sitting in the chair before the fireplace, wearing reading glasses, an open book on his lap. He had apparently not heard her come in, for as she opened her mouth to greet him he suddenly swore softly and with an abrupt, angry movement, tossed the book on the floor, where it skidded facedown into the hearth. The glasses were hurled across the room after it and bounced on the carpet but, miraculously, did not break, and then he leaned back in the chair, pressing his fingers viciously into his temples.

"Is that any way to treat a book?" she exclaimed, coming into the room.

His eyes were unfocused when he first looked at her, and then his expression quickly changed to a defensive scowl. "What are you doing here?" he demanded. "I have a splitting headache."

Jennifer lifted an eyebrow mildly, and he turned his face impatiently away from her. She was not certain whether the anger was directed at himself or at her, and she suspected it was an equal mixture. She picked up the book and placed it on the table with the others. "I'll get you an aspirin," she volunteered quietly.

"Don't bother." His tone was short and clipped.

"It won't help. Nothing helps. There's not a damn thing you or I or the government of the United States can do about it, so just leave me alone, will you?"

Jennifer stared at him, a chill penetrating the puzzled protest that had accompanied the beginning of his statement. "I don't understand. Do you have a lot of headaches? What has the government got to do with—"

The look that flashed across his eyes was too swift to be fear, too intense to be reticence. He looked quickly away from her again, and she could see the muscle in his jaw tighten. "Forget it," he said briefly.

She watched him cautiously. "I didn't mean for you to read them all in one night," she ventured mildly, gesturing toward the stack of books. "No due date. Take a month, or a year...."

"I don't have a year!" he shouted at her, the anger in his tone and his face completely inappropriate for the situation. She paused, staring at him, and immediately he looked as though he regretted his outburst. His face tightened into a defensive mask, and his fingers curled around the arms of the chair as though to forcefully repress the anger that still churned within him. Adam turned his face away.

"There are other libraries," she told him quietly, trying to inject a note of humor into the situation. "Even other librarians who are just as generous with their lending privileges as I am. Just because you're leaving here—"

"You don't understand," he interrupted tersely, not looking at her. "Time is running out, I don't have—" And then he broke off suddenly. It was a moment before he spoke again, and he still refused to look at her. "Forget it," he said. "It's a stupid conversation. I'm sorry I threw the book, and I'm sorry I snapped at you, okay? Just forget it."

But Jennifer didn't want to forget it. A sort of creeping dread had come over her that was a result of both what he had said and what he had not said; it frightened her. But it was obvious he was going to say no more: Once again his secret torments would remain his own; he was locked into an exclusive world she could not enter. That was frustrating; it hurt her and angered her more than she wanted to admit, for she had no reason to want to get involved with him and his problems. He was a stranger brought into her life by nothing more than a capricious shift of circumstances, and when he recovered his health, the chances were very good that he would leave and she would never see or hear from him again. Yet...he would haunt her. That she knew already. What was it he had said? *It's hard not to get involved with you....* Jennifer realized with a start that she had been involved with him, too, from the moment their hands had touched and sparks flown—a portent of things to come? It was irrational, it was unexpected, Jennifer was not even certain she liked it, but yes, she was involved with him... more than she had ever thought possible.

She was disturbed by this realization, and she turned away, not wanting him to see the expression on her face. She picked up his glasses and said in a falsely casual tone, "You're lucky they weren't broken. They look expensive."

"They are," he returned briefly, and when she put the glasses silently on the mantel, he turned to look at her, a slowly softening apology easing away the lines on his face. "I've done it again, haven't I?" he said ruefully. "Taken out my troubles on you. And here I was determined to impress you with what a likable character I am when I'm not hurt or delirious or soaked and freezing."

Jennifer couldn't help smiling, mostly because that haunted look had disappeared from his face. She hated it when the look was there, loved it when it was gone. She challenged him pertly, "All right, I'm ready. Impress me."

He smiled too, and unexpectedly extended his hand for her. It was such a natural gesture of open friendship that she responded immediately, coming over to him and dropping to the rug at his feet when his fingers took hers lightly. "I try not to be moody, Jenny," he said. His eyes were lowered to his hand, which held the tips of her fingers very lightly, as though expecting her at any moment to pull away. "Most of the time I'm not, and that's the truth. It's only when I'm up against something I can't control that I get angry." He spoke absently, almost to himself, and as he did his index finger slowly moved to caress the smooth knuckles of her hand. It was perhaps no more than an automatic gesture, not meant to be intimate or affectionate, but it made Jennifer's pulse race and a quick awareness open up inside her. She kept her eyes fixed on his face, which was reflective and bent at an absorbed angle toward the joining of their hands, and she did not move or speak for fear of spoiling the moment. "Like being sick and helpless," he went on softly. "Like being caught in a storm. . . . Like the things you do to me whenever I'm around you."

She was so startled she could hardly speak, and perhaps it would have been best if she had said nothing at all. But of all the things she might have expected him to say, that was not among them, and she could not prevent a stammered, "M-me? What do I do?"

He released her hand and looked at her soberly. "Right now," he said, "you make me want to kiss you. The night of the storm you made me want to make love to you, and that's why I was angry—not with you, but with myself, because I knew if I had stayed, I would have made love to you, and I don't want to have an affair with you, Jenny."

She had to look away. Her heart was thundering and her cheeks were tingling and she was not certain whether this reaction was from anticipation or surprise—or perhaps disappointment—because he sat there so close, the tender, sincere words still echoing about them, and he made no move to touch her. She wanted him to touch her; she had waited for his touch since their first meeting, and now she had to admit to herself that if he had stayed that night—if circumstances had been different and he had tried to make love to her—she would have probably ended up sharing her bed and not regretting a moment of it. The realization only made her color deepen and her pulse rate increase, because Jennifer had never considered herself a woman of easy affection, and she certainly never before would have envisioned herself in bed with a man she hardly knew. Yet from the first moment she had sensed something different about him, something that made him seem more than a stranger to her, something that pulled her to him and made her want to be close to him.... But it was all too much. The more she was with him the more confused she became, and she really did not know him at all. She had no intention of pursuing this conversation or of encouraging the mood that surrounded them, which suddenly seemed fraught with emotional dangers, and she made a deliberate attempt to calm the uneven rhythm of her heart and subdue her betraying color as she looked back at him and smiled.

"Dr. Thompson wants to see you in his office this afternoon," she said. "Do you feel strong enough to make the trip?"

He accepted her signal to change the subject, but she could not be certain whether the expression that crossed his face was disappointment or gratitude. "Sheer willpower has prompted me toward a miraculous recovery," he answered, and a teasing grin played at the corner of his lips as he added, "That, and the supernatural healing magic of the local witch. What time am I supposed to be there?"

"Whenever you're ready," she said, getting to her feet. She tried to make the movement seem a natural extension of the conversation and not a gesture signifying the end of a moment of intimacy that was so poignant it still clung to her like the bittersweet memory of a nostalgic perfume.

"I'll shower and change." He paused at the entrance to the hall, his expression light and relaxed. "Do your nursing duties include making the trip with me, or does this mean I'm on my own from here on out?"

"My nursing duties," she informed him, "include driving you into town—provided you trust me with your truck, of course."

He hesitated. "I thought you said you couldn't drive."

"I said I *didn't* drive," she corrected. "I've had a license since I was eighteen."

That seemed to satisfy him, and he was perfectly willing to turn over the keys to the Blazer to her when he returned, showered, shaved, and dressed most attractively in brown corduroys and a gold turtleneck that very nearly matched the color of his hair.

When Dr. Thompson had finished his examination of Adam, he called Jennifer into his office. At first she was surprised, but she should have known better than to think he merely wanted to discuss the progress of their mutual "patient."

"You're a good nurse." He smiled at her by way of easing into the subject. "Your young man is making a fine recovery. No complications from the fever, and the arm will be as good as new before Christmas."

"He's not my 'young man,'" Jennifer felt compelled to point out, but the doctor merely lifted an eyebrow mildly and gestured that she be seated. When she took her place in the worn green leather chair in which she had sat so many times before, he went around the desk, scribbled a few notes on what she assumed to be Adam's chart, and then leaned back in his chair and simply looked at her for a moment.

"What I really want to know," he said, just as she expected, "is how you're doing."

"Fine," she assured him. "Really."

"Any more episodes since I last saw you?"

Jennifer was not really antagonistic toward her doctor, and she tried to subdue the automatic flare of irritation she felt whenever anyone brought up the subject of her "condition." Dr. Thompson had been remarkably supportive throughout her entire ordeal, and when she had come to the decision a year ago to try to live her life without the medication he had so diligently prescribed since she was three years old, he had backed her up without a word of reprimand or discouragement. In fact, his was the only support she had gotten on that particular decision, and she was grateful to him. She never lied to him. "One," she admitted. "During the accident the night that Adam hurt his arm. But it wasn't bad," she added quickly. "It didn't last long, and I felt fine afterward. . . ."

He nodded, watching her. "Did you drive today, Jenny?"

She sudued a flush of guilt. "What else could I do?" she defended herself. "He couldn't drive with his arm, and besides, I did fine. I really think I'm getting better, Doctor."

"Now, Jenny," he said patiently, "we've been over this too many times. This isn't a disease for which there is a cure; it's a condition you'll just have to learn to live with. You're not going to get better, Jenny; that's something you're going to have to remind yourself of every single day, because when you start forgetting, you're asking for trouble."

"I know," she said quietly, dropping her eyes. "And I do." But then she met his eyes again evenly. "But you're the one who told me not to be afraid to live a normal life, and that's what I'm doing. I thought about the danger of driving, and you know I don't do it often. Even you said it should be perfectly safe to drive around town as long as there was someone in the car with me."

"Someone who knows about your condition," he pointed out. "Does Adam?"

Once again she dropped her eyes. "No," she admitted.

He was silent for a time. When next he spoke his tone was deceptively casual. "How long is he planning to stay with us, do you know?"

"No," she answered, on easier ground now. "He paid a month in advance for the house, but he never said anything about staying longer than that...." She smiled a little ruefully. "After the way his visit started off, he may decide the sooner he puts this place behind him, the better. I can't say that I'd blame him." But even as she spoke she knew she hoped desperately that would not be the case. Already it seemed impossible that he could just walk out of her life in another day, week...even a month.

As though reading her thoughts, the doctor said tactfully, "I imagine you two have become rather ... close, through all of this."

Jennifer answered warily, "I suppose. We're friends, if that's what you mean. And we're neighbors. It's only right that we should—"

He held up his hand and smiled. "You don't have to defend anything to me. Of course it's only natural. I was only going to say," he added, sobering, "that before you become any more involved, you should tell him."

Jennifer did not know what to say. She had no secrets from Dr. Thompson and her trust in him was implicit. He was discreet and nonjudgmental, and she had no fear of sharing anything with him. Such was the nature of their relationship that he had prescribed contraceptives for her without her asking before she went away for college and had kept the prescription refilled since then with no questions asked. There had been no need for them to discuss whether or not Jennifer needed such protection; the doctor assumed she would lead a normal life, and they each understood the risks of an unplanned pregnancy where there was a possibility of transmitting a congenital disease. Probably he was concerned now about the extent of her intimacy with Adam for exactly that reason, but there really was nothing to tell. She knew he was right, if quite a bit premature. In all likelihood the necessity for confiding in Adam would never arise; they had no relationship beyond that of neighbors and probably never would.... She conveniently ignored the events of a few hours ago and her own emotions, which were trying to tell her otherwise.

She took up her purse and smiled at him as she started to rise. "Anything else?"

"I'll take the stitches out in a couple of weeks," the doctor said, walking her to the door. "By that time," he added pointedly, "he should be able to drive."

Jennifer gave him a clear, understanding smile. "Right," she said.

"That was very ominous," Adam commented as they walked back to the truck. "Doesn't the doctor usually only call in the loved ones to tell them how long the patient has to live?" But behind the light comment he looked uneasy, and that disturbed Jennifer.

She laughed. "Not necessarily. In your case the only message I have," she added with a meaningful sidelong glance at him, "is that you mend your foolish ways."

"Such as?" He held open the door for her before going around to the passenger side.

"Such as getting caught in storms, inviting infections, staying in unheated houses, and...." She glanced at him once again as she switched on the ignition. "Staying up all night reading, when you need all the sleep you can get to recover your strength."

"Who says I stayed up all night?" he challenged curiously.

Jennifer was embarrassed to have been caught spying, but she had to admit, "I saw your lights on."

Now he seemed embarrassed, but he shrugged it off with a slightly crooked grin. "It's a bad habit. Nights were the worst in Nam, and since then I leave lights on all the time. It's stupid, I know, but I never realized before how much I took electric light for granted."

Jennifer could understand that, and he read it in her face. He relaxed, resting an arm across the back of the seat, the sleeve of his injured arm pushed up above the fresh bandage and resting in his lap. Jennifer was pleased that the day's exercise had not seemed to take too much out of him. His face was still very pale and those hideous dark circles still lined his eyes, but he looked comfortable and alert and, in fact, unsettlingly attractive in the tight-fitting sweater and casual jeans. Jennifer turned her eyes deliberately back to the road as he inquired casually, "Did you ever finish *Elias Cotton*?"

"Yes," Jennifer answered enthusiastically. "You were right; it was as good all the way through as it started out. It has definitely earned a recommended reading spot on the new fiction shelf of the library."

"I thought you'd like it," he said.

"I could identify with it," she admitted. "Not with the character, precisely, but with his conflicts and decisions...which I suppose are common to everyone. It seems to me that each of us, eventually, must reach a point in our lives when we have to back off and take a second look, face what we are and the hand life has dealt us and accept it."

The casual tone of his voice belied the intent look he gave her. "You've done that?"

"Yes," she said softly, thinking about her decision a year ago. And then, with sudden insight, she glanced at him. "Is that what you're doing now? Is that what this pilgrimage of yours across the country with your camera is about?"

Adam looked very thoughtful. Jennifer could feel his eyes on her even when she turned her own carefully back to the road. "I never really thought about it like that," he admitted. "I suppose it is. And when you stop and—take this second look," he inquired, "what happens then? Where do you go from there?"

"Either forward or backward," Jennifer answered. "You can't stand still. Hopefully, like Elias, you accept what you see—you don't have to like it, but you accept it—and you find the courage to be honest about it, with yourself and others." Unbidden the doctor's words about telling Adam came back to her, but she pushed the memory away quickly. This was neither the time nor the place.

"That's the hardest part, isn't it?" said Adam reflectively, almost to himself. "Being honest about it."

"Yes," was all Jennifer could reply, and silence fell.

Adam said suddenly, "Can you pull over here for a minute?"

Jennifer slowed the truck. "What's wrong?"

"Nothing. I just want to look." He leaned forward as she stopped the car and pointed toward the church steeple in the distance. It stood like a white finger etched against a blinding cobalt sky, the setting sun a golden ball that rested upon its tip. The sparkling glow spilled down upon the bare treetops and made them look as though they were drawn in silver paint, reflecting their radiance back toward the sky and downward in stark definitive shadows that lay like entwining black threads upon the streets and the roofs of houses. "It's funny," he said softly. "I've seen it before—I even took a picture of it—but I didn't see anything beautiful in it then." He looked at her and smiled. "Maybe everything looks different to me when you're around."

She smiled a little uncertainly, aware again of the portentous speeding of her heart, the urge to touch him or to be touched by him, to share the moment in a physical as well as an emotional way. But caution dictated that she turn her eyes back to the view. "It's a shame you don't have your camera now."

"It's all right," he said. "It's already recorded where it really matters—in my head. The camera sees for other people; the important thing is what I see for myself." The reflective tone in his voice was expelled with his sigh as he sat back. Jennifer noticed a barely perceptible tightening of the muscles of his face; she sensed a swift intensity about him that started the anxiety in the pit of her stomach again. "Don't you see what I mean about time slipping away?" he demanded impatiently. "All that I've missed this past week...it will never come again. Even now the sun will never strike that steeple in exactly the same way again; the shadows won't fall at precisely that angle tomorrow.... It will all be gone, and if I hadn't been here to see it, I would never have another chance."

She could not keep the puzzlement out of her tone or her expression. She had never known anyone who reacted to the simple things of life so intensely, so wholeheartedly, and that propensity both fascinated and frightened her. "That's not scientifically true, you know," she said. "Next year on this date at precisely the same moment the sun will be in exactly the same position. You may not be here to see it, but there's always a second chance."

"Not for me there's not," he said quietly. Jennifer thought he was hardly aware of speaking out loud. "Next year will be too late." But then he recovered himself, looked at her quickly, and said abruptly, "Let's go home."

He was silent until she parked the truck at the side of his house, and Jennifer was afraid he was slipping into another one of his bouts of moodiness. She was relieved when he dispelled that notion by getting out of the truck and greeting Bear exuberantly, then looking up at her with a grin. "What are you fixing me for dinner?" he demanded. "I'm starved."

Jennifer's brows flew up in mock indignation. "So now I'm your cook, am I? There's nothing like taking a little neighborly kindness for granted. Maybe I'll just leave you to fix your own dinner." And she turned to flounce away.

He caught her arm, laughing. "Forgive me; I'm a chauvinist at heart." When he pulled her around to face him, her own eyes were dancing, which evoked a quick flickering of response in his. As he looked at her the laughter died into something else—something so much like tenderness that Jennifer caught her breath, and it seemed that every fiber of her being leaped to respond to that quiet look. Slowly he brought his hand up; he touched her jaw lightly, tracing its curve until his fingers rested upon the birthmark at her chin. "I could never take you for granted, Jennifer," he said softly.

His hand released her arm and moved as though to encircle her waist; she thought his face might have moved just a fraction of an inch closer and his eyes were heavy with an intent she could not misread. But in the half second that indecision hovered, instinct took over, and Jennifer stepped away quickly. "All right, you win," she said somewhat breathlessly. "One dinner coming up."

The expression that crossed his face might have been confusion, but it was covered quickly with a smile. He followed her into the house.

Later Jennifer would wonder why she had spoiled that moment when she knew that what she wanted above all else was to be kissed by him, but the answer was not too difficult to find. He had said it himself this afternoon—he did not want to have an affair with her. Jennifer was not the type of girl who had affairs, and that was not what she wanted from him either...at least she did not think so. How could she be sure of anything when he was constantly changing and contradicting himself? One moment he was light-hearted and relaxed with her and the next he was cold and distant. In one breath he could go from tender affection to irrational anger, and she never knew whether he saw her as a friend or an enemy. He said he wanted to make love to her, but he did not want to have an affair with her. He said he wanted to kiss her, but he wouldn't. What would she be letting herself in for if she became any more involved with him? He was a man so filled with inconsistencies and hidden motives that she could not even be sure of her own emotions any-more. What *did* he want from her?

And more importantly, what did she want?

Though she tried to talk him into something more substantial for dinner, he insisted upon nothing more filling than an omelet. He built a fire in the fireplace and they ate sitting upon the hearth rug before it, not talking much, sharing a silence that should have been awkward but wasn't.

"I'm glad at least Bear appreciates my cook-ing," she commented dryly as she watched him feed the remaining half of his omelet to the dog.

He grinned quite endearingly. "I guess I should have waited until you went home to do that," he apologized. "And it's no reflection on your cook-ing; it was delicious. The only thing missing was a good wine. I'll have to remember to pick some up the next time I'm in town."

"I'll be glad to bring back anything you need," Jennifer volunteered, taking the dishes to the sink. "I know you didn't have much time to lay in supplies before you got sick. Just make me a list."

"That's okay; I'll be able to drive next week. And," he added with a quirk of his brow as she returned, "you've done a pretty good job of stocking my cupboards—which I appreciate, by the way."

She lifted her shoulders in a shrug and dropped to the hearth rug beside him again. "All in the line of duty," she said.

He looked at her; the firelight played in his eyes, making them seem almost translucent. "I like the way you execute your duties," he said. "In fact..." His hand brushed across her own hand, where it rested beside his on the floor, touched the curve of her elbow, moved inexorably to her throat. "I like everything about you."

"Is that right?" Though her breath suddenly seemed to be shortened and her heart had leaped into a suddenly escalated rhythm, her voice sounded almost normal. "You could have fooled me."

Adam smiled with vague affection, and his thumb moved upward to caress the area near her earlobe. The awareness of his touch spread downward to her fingertips, opening every cell of her body along its course and drawing a tight pulse of anticipation to the area just below her breastbone. The shadows of the fire cast his face into a rosy hue and disguised the lines of stress and illness that had been there, highlighting the lean planes and the soft curve of his lips, reflecting the gold of his shirt in his eyes and his hair. His fingers were a blush of warmth against her throat, and the soft circular motion of his thumb near her ear sensuously hypnotic. He said softly, "I explained that. And apologized for it. Besides, that was then."

"And now?" It was barely a whisper. Her eyes, wide and luminous in the radiant light, searched his face anxiously. His own eyes moved over her face with more leisure, pausing over each feature and studying it before they moved on, and the expression within their depths told her nothing—except that he wanted at that moment exactly what she did.

"Now..." he said, and the motion of his thumb ceased. The fingers that had caressed her throat moved upward to cup her chin, where they applied a barely perceptible pressure that tilted her face toward him. Once more his eyes swept her face and rested at last upon her lips. "Now I've decided to take your advice and face the facts, to be honest with myself, and with you—as much as I can, as much as you can take...." And with each phrase, each word, his face moved fractionally, almost hesitantly, closer, until it filled her entire vision. She saw his eyelids close just before her own did, and then his lips closed gently upon hers.

Jennifer had never been kissed like that before. Never a romantic, she had not passed her life in fanciful waiting for the kiss of a prince to bring her to life. In her limited experience during adolescence, and later in the more sophisticated world of the state university, she had never grown to think of any one man's kiss as very much different from another's.... But Jennifer knew the mo-

ment Adam's lips met hers that this was different,
it was as though there was something deep within
the heart of every woman that lay dormant until it
was awakened by the kiss of one very special
man. . . . And for her this was the kiss. And Adam
Wilson was the man.

It started out softly, a breathless taste of wonder that had been too long postponed, and it was
sweet, like the first taste of candy on Christmas
morning. Perhaps he would have left it at that.
Perhaps he would have moved away after that
first gentle clasping, but Jennifer's response was
inevitable. The surprise of it, the utter wonder of
it, caught her completely off guard. Instincts
ruled, and the first taste was not enough; like a
greedy child too long denied, she wanted more;
she was not aware of nor could she have prevented the arm that crept slowly about his neck,
the parting of her lips beneath his on a choked
breath, and that was the signal that released a
slowly building dam of passion within him. His
hand left her face and moved downward and
around, circling her waist and pressing her closer
to him; he shifted his body so that one leg encir-
cled both of hers and her chest met his. She could
feel the pounding of his heart against her breast
with the steadily increasing pressure that brought
her closer and the heat that flared in his face and
radiated from the hard fingers against her spine.

His kiss was powerful and demanding, tasting
her urgently, sweeping her lips and her teeth and
the corners of her mouth with his tongue, and

Jennifer was helpless against the fire the contact was generating. She could only respond with instincts and needs she had never before known she possessed, her fingers tightening against the strong column of his neck beneath his hair, her mouth opening beneath his in insistent urging to receive the warm invasion of his tongue, and then her heart was slamming against her ribs so hard it was frightening, her skin was blistering with the roar of the hot flush that swept through her, she couldn't breathe. She didn't know herself anymore.

She had never known she was capable of such emotions; it almost seemed as though someone else were inhabiting her body and being swept away by these mindless sensations of need and desire. . . . Her limbs were weak and watery, incapable of movement or response; they hardly seemed to belong to her at all. She thought nothing, she felt nothing, but the intensity of this moment and the need to have it go on forever; she felt herself becoming lost in him. And all she knew was that she wanted him, now and forever; she wanted to draw him close and become a part of him, and it seemed as though it had always been that way.

He moved his lips to the corner of her mouth, then to her cheek. His breath was rapid and hot and uneven; it matched the rhythm of her own. The muscles of the arm that strained around his neck began to tremble, and the weak, quivery feeling moved from the inside out so that her entire body seemed to be racked with a series of fine, delicate shivers. The thundering of her heart was deafening, and when she opened her eyes the entire room seemed to pulse in time with it.

His hand moved upward along the course of her spine, threading through the thick pony tail that began at the nape of her neck, gathering its silken luster between his fingers and letting it fall again with a feathery warmth against her back. His lips touched hers again in a bare whisper and then closed lovingly over the birthmark on her chin. "Jennifer," he whispered. His cheek rested against hers, soft and warm against the raw flame that burned in her face; he nuzzled the inviting curve between her neck and her shoulder, and the fan of his breath across her ear made her shiver. She tried to steady her breath, and she groped blindly for a grasp on a situation fast escalating out of control, but all the time her fingers were moving through the thick, soft texture of his hair and exploring the sharp angles of his neck and jaw, and she really did not want reason to return. She wanted no more than this moment....

His face moved slowly down until his cheek rested against the small rounded curve of her breast; she caught her breath sharply as his hand came up to gently cup its shape. And as she waited, suspended and aching with anticipation, he turned his face and pressed his lips against the wool-covered softness there, his hot breath penetrating the material and jolting new nerve endings into painful awareness. With a muffled moan she dropped her face to his hair and in shaky breaths inhaled the clean fragrance of him; he was aware only of the movements of his lips, which now traveled upward to her throat, and his fingers, which spread over the thrusting point of her breast, finding and caressing its throbbing center. All of her was filled with him, all of her mind and all of her yearning; there seemed in that moment to exist nothing in her life outside of him... and then she felt his tensing, the slow careful intake of his breath, the change come over him. His hand dropped to her waist, and he drew her to him tightly, almost fiercely, as though for the last time, and his voice was a low groan muffled against her neck. "Ah, Jenny," he said despairingly. "What have we started?"

Her breath caught in her throat, and the sound it made there was like a little sob as he moved away. The absence of him throbbed throughout every fiber of her body like a million tiny knife wounds as he turned his back on her, propping his fist upon his upraised knee and pressing his forehead to it. The sound of his unsteady breathing was audible even above her own. She saw the straining of his back muscles through the tight-fitting sweater, and she yearned to touch him, to ease the tension and the distress away and, in the process, to push away the terrifying pain that was growing within her with the certainty of his presence... but she couldn't. His very posture rejected her, and an awful, aching loneliness engulfed her—his and her own—and it was made all the worse because she did not understand the reason for it.

He said dully, "You should have stopped me."

She could not lie. How could she, when she had already told him in the irrefutable language of her body the depths of her emotions and the truth of her desires? Tears pricked her eyelids, but she hardly noticed them. Her voice trembled as she answered, very softly, "I didn't want to."

He turned; he looked at her, and the quick light of wonder and hope in his eyes seemed to her at that moment a reason for living. He wasn't sorry. He didn't regret it. His eyes moved over her face, quickly at first, then more slowly, and the reluctant expression that crossed his features seemed both a promise and a sorrow.

"Adam," she said quickly, and with difficulty, "if...if you're worried about my getting pregnant—"

"No," he said immediately, and she believed him. "No, it's not that." It was something deeper, more important, more frightening for Jennifer. The struggle to tell it showed in his eyes. "That's not...what I meant," he said, and his voice and his expression were filled with misery. "I..."

For a moment she thought he would not go on. She saw his fists tighten, though his resolve seemed weak.

"Jenny," he began haltingly. His voice was hoarse, and the sudden intense urgency in his eyes arrested her. Unconsciously her hands clenched, and she waited, straining for what it was he was about to say, knowing instinctively it would be the most important thing of her life. "I have to tell you...."

And perhaps she had known he wouldn't finish. He dropped his eyes, and when he looked back at her, there was reluctance in them, but underscored with an undeniable firmness. "You'd better go home," he said quietly.

She nodded. There was nothing else she could do. Somehow she found strength in her legs, and she got to her feet, grateful that he was too involved with his own misery to notice the clumsiness of her movements or the unsteadiness of her breath.

He said without looking at her, "Don't be angry."

"I'm not," she managed, very softly and rather raggedly, and she meant it. In some way the past few moments seemed to have taken their relationship onto a plane where anger was not a conceivable emotion—it seemed pale and childish and totally inappropriate in light of the things she had just learned she was capable of feeling for him. She did not think she could ever be angry with him.

As she reached the door his voice stopped her. "Jenny," he said. She turned and saw the sadness in his eyes, the ghost of an absent smile on his lips. It was as though he had looked into the future and come away with a bittersweet memory; its mark had left a furrow of pain on his brow and the taste of something sweet on his lips. It was as though he had faced the inevitable—not liking it, perhaps, but he had faced it—and accepted it. He said quietly, "It's not going to go away, is it?"

She answered softly, barely audibly, "No." And she left.

Chapter Six

Jennifer did not go back to Adam's house for the next few days. Once again the first move had to be made by him, but it was not like the last time, when anger, tension, and a misunderstanding had kept them apart. It was not as though they deliberately tried to avoid each other—although Jennifer was tempted to do just that on one or two occasions. Bear greeted her as customary in the mornings, and as likely as not his master was someplace close behind; he might call out a friendly "Good morning" or lift his hand in a noncommittal wave. On Sunday he spent almost the entire day out of doors, venturing into the woods with his camera or simply sitting by the lake enjoying the view, and when Jennifer went outside to empty the trash or bring in firewood, he did not pretend to ignore her; he called hello, but that was all. Jennifer assumed he was attempting to establish a new pattern for their relationship—that of being neighbors and nothing more—and she was not quite certain how she felt about that.

The entire encounter with Adam Wilson had

turned her sense of values and her opinion of herself inside out. She had never before thought of herself as being the type of woman who became romantically or passionately involved with enigmatic strangers. She did not have brief encounters or sophisticated, open-ended relationships, and she had never before let her heart rule her head. Yet this *was* a matter of the heart, the first one she had ever known, and it could not be judged by normal standards.

He did not want to get involved with her. He had made that clear. He had told her bluntly and without hesitation that he did not want to have an affair with her, so what had their last evening together been? A moment of weakness on his part, a matter of convenience? She did not think so. She couldn't believe that. Not when she remembered the look in his eyes, the broken tone of his voice when he had asked her to go. She sometimes suspected that it had taken as much courage for him to start what had happened between them as it had taken to end it, and that was not the behavior of a man who gave in to fleeting impulses. Something was happening between them, and she knew it was as powerful on his part as it was on hers, and completely out of their control. She did not know what to do about it. She was not even sure whether she wanted to do anything at all.

Late Tuesday afternoon as she emerged from the path that opened behind her house his voice startled her. "Hello, beautiful lady! Don't move." She laughed and threw up her hand to cover her face as the shutter of his camera began clicking.

"Is this what you do all day?" she challenged. "Lie in wait with your camera until some unsuspecting victim comes out of the woods and then scare them to death? Stop that; you're wasting film!"

He lowered the camera with a grin. "You make me sound like the troll under the bridge. And I don't lie in wait for just any unsuspecting victim—only beautiful wood nymphs."

Wonderful pleasure flowed through her like warm syrup; it was reflected by the glow of the sun and shone in her face. "So now I'm a wood nymph, am I? What happened to the witch?"

He stepped forward and took a length of her golden red hair between his fingers, spreading it over his palm like a swatch of translucent silk. His eyes widened and lightened with pleasure as he watched the play of the sun upon its strands, and he said, "She's still lurking below the surface somewhere, I suspect, weaving her spell even as I speak. Your hair is so pretty." He lifted his palm so that the breeze caught the strands it supported and fluttered them loose over her shoulder again. He was smiling, his eyes clear and bright and heart-stoppingly tender. "When I was a child I had a book of illustrated fairy stories, and Rapunzel's hair was just this color. I never thought it could be real. But then, you've shown me a lot of things the past two weeks that I never thought could be real."

"My," she said lightly, somewhat breathlessly. "We do wax poetic this evening, don't we?"

His smile only deepened and caught sun-sparks

in his eyes. "How could I not, living in fairyland under the spell of a combination witch-wood nymph and Greek goddess for all I know?"

She laughed. "Now that is stretching a point, isn't it? Greek goddess?"

The corners of his eyes crinkled delightfully, dispelling less attractive lines in a motion. At the moment he looked very young, carefree, light-hearted. The few days he had spent in the autumn sun had already brought a glow of health to his face, softening its former harshness and even minimizing the dark pockets of sleeplessness that circled his eyes. If it had been sheer willpower that had prompted such a remarkable recovery, then he had a great deal of willpower indeed, and it made Jennifer feel warm all over simply to see him look so well.

He turned with an expansive gesture and declared, "Did you conjure up this incredible autumn weather we've been having just for me? If so, I thank you. Have you ever seen days so bright or air so clear? And the colors—they have a life of their own. I can focus my camera on a single spot and it won't take the same picture from one moment to the next. There's movement and life everywhere."

His rich mood flowed through Jennifer like an intoxicating tonic, buoying her and lifting her up to his plane, where everything seemed brighter and clearer and more alive simply because he saw it that way. "I wish I could take the credit," she said, and laughed. "With glowing reviews like that I could go into business for myself—if someone else hadn't already cornered the market, of course."

In an easy, natural movement, his hand fell upon her shoulder, and they started walking toward the lake. "I saw a flock of geese flying over today," he said. "They were so beautiful I forgot to get my camera. It's just as well, I suppose— some things are simply too perfect to be captured. The picture will never be as beautiful as the memory. When do you usually get your first snow?"

"By Thanksgiving," she answered, "unless it's going to be a mild winter." And she hesitated, almost afraid to ask the next question. "Do you ... think you'll be here then?"

"Sometimes," he answered quietly, his eyes squinted toward the shiny reflection of the lake, "I think I could stay here forever." Then, almost before hope could register, he asked, "What about the lake? Does it freeze enough for skating?"

"Sometimes, by January or February. It's pretty deep in the middle, though, we always stay near the edge." She wanted desperately to ask if he would be here then, but she did not dare. It was too much to hope for, and she would rather not know.

"Your sister came by today," he said unexpectedly, and there was a speculative twinkle in his eye as he glanced down at her. "She brought me a Dutch apple pie, still warm from the oven. And I always thought New Englanders were very reserved and unfriendly."

This came as a surprise to Jennifer, although she should have known Jo would not be able to restrain her curiosity much longer; she supposed she should count herself lucky her sister had not made a surprise visit to the newest member of the community sooner. "They are also very nosy," responded Jennifer dryly. "Did she manage to drag your entire life story out of you?"

"Pretty much," he admitted cheerfully. "But the pie was worth it."

"Jo Ellen's pies are the secret of her success," agreed Jennifer. "If she were an ambitious woman, she could have the major powers of the world at her command."

"There's about half of it left," he suggested easily. "Care to help me finish it off?"

Jennifer tried to subdue the sudden clench of anticipation in the pit of her stomach that had nothing whatsoever to do with apple pie. He had made the first move. But toward what? She disguised her nervousness with pretended surprise. "Before dinner?"

"How about after dinner?" He made the invitation sound casual, though they both knew it was not. Without waiting for her response he turned and began leading her with an arm about her shoulders toward his house. "I owe you one, after all, and I'd like a chance to match my culinary skills against yours."

"Why do I get the feeling I'm about to come out second best in a contest of bachelor cookery?" she responded dryly, but her heart was leaping and cascading in a joyous rhythm, and happiness was building inside her like a bubble ready to burst.

In the kitchen Jennifer teased him that anyone could broil a steak, and he should have chosen something more challenging if he intended to impress her with his skill.

"Ah, but it takes a very special talent to coax flavor and succulence out of what is, after all, no more than a dead cow," he replied, and she giggled. "Besides," he admitted. "It's the only thing I know how to make. The salad is up to you—you know where the refrigerator is."

"I should have guessed," she responded in mock resignation, and slid off the stool. "And here I was thinking this was one night I would get out of cooking."

"I told you; I'm a chauvinist at heart—and also very lazy. You've spoiled me."

But for Jennifer spoiling him had been a labor of love, one she had never had the opportunity to perform before. He had brought so much into her life without trying, without, perhaps, wanting to. She wished she had the courage to tell him so, but she was too afraid of rejection to try.

He had purchased a bottle of red wine—the imported variety that was not available in town—and as he poured it she commented, "Does all this finery mean you've been feeling well enough to drive?"

"Oh, sure. Your magic potions have worked wonders." He lit candles at the kitchen table and gestured her to be seated as he brought their plates. "The arm still hurts," he admitted, "and I guess it will for a while, but it's nothing I can't live with."

"You're a very determined man," Jennifer said. "Another person would have used an injury like that as an excuse to pamper and feel sorry for himself for another two months."

"Feeling sorry for myself is an exercise I've indulged in quite enough of late, thank you," he answered. "Try the steak."

She tasted it thoughtfully, and then commented, "Not bad. Not bad at all...." Her eyes twinkled. "For a dead cow."

He made a face and threatened her playfully with his knife.

Dinner was lighthearted and easy, a welcome change of pace from their usual encounters. But Jennifer was so happy simply to be with him, to see him feeling so well and so at ease, that she did not really do justice to the meal. She ended up slipping scraps to Bear under the table when she thought she was unobserved, and Adam remarked calmly, "Am I to take that as a reflection on my cooking, or is this just your subtle way of getting back at me for all your efforts that have—in a phrase—gone to the dogs?"

She pretended to be chagrined. "I couldn't help it," she defended herself. "He was looking at me with those big brown eyes...."

"Oh, yes," said Adam softly, and she knew perfectly well he was no longer talking about the dog. "I know all about big brown eyes and the crazy things they can make us do."

Jennifer dropped her gaze quickly, afraid to try

to read what was in his own eyes. "Besides," she said, "you cook like a typical man. You make entirely too much for the normal person to eat."

"Does that mean we should save the pie for later?" He got up and took their dishes to the sink, scraping the leftovers into a bowl for Bear. "I'll put some coffee on; you go on into the living room and sit down. I've got a fire going."

The fire was beginning to die down, and by the time Jennifer had stoked it to a cheerful blaze again, he was returning from the kitchen with two glasses of wine. As she straightened up to meet him she was surprised by a peculiarly reflective expression on his face—surprised and arrested. He looked at her with the experienced eye of an artist assessing and absorbing every detail from head to foot, and his eyes reflected nothing but appreciation for what they saw. He looked at her, she realized suddenly, the same way he had looked at the church steeple that day, and at the lake this afternoon—as though he were memorizing and storing the memory for a later day. That started a small knot of pain deep within her that she tried to ignore, for it only reminded her that he would not be here forever, and that soon everything about this place—herself included—would be nothing more than a memory to him.

And then he said unexpectedly, "Do you know what I like about you? You always wear dresses, or skirts. So few women do anymore."

She laughed a trifle uncomfortably. "You just wait until winter really hits. Then all my feminine skirts go into storage, and you won't see me in anything but wool slacks and snowsuits and three pairs of socks underneath.'' But would he? She wondered. Would he even be here then?

Once again he looked her over thoughtfully. "You know what I don't like about you? Those boots. They ruin the whole effect."

"They're warm," she said to justify them.

"Sit down." Adam placed the wineglasses on the mantel and knelt before her when she sat on the sofa. "It's plenty warm in here; you may as well be comfortable."

"I am comfortable," she protested, but he slid her boots easily from her stocking-covered feet, first one, then the other. He held her left foot in his hand just a moment longer than was necessary, his fingers caressing her ankle and warm palms cupping her heel in a way that sent warm shivers upward, and then he released it, smiling, and he got up to sit beside her. "You have pretty feet," he said.

"They're too big," she answered, and then, moving the discussion delicately away from her anatomy, she inquired, "I've just been wondering—what will your friend who's writing the book say when all the pictures you send him are of one particular rustic New England lake?"

He shrugged lightly, resting his arm along the back of the sofa. "Actually, I've already gotten most of the pictures I need for him. New England was my last stop before Canada, and to tell you the truth I couldn't have picked a place more representative of the whole of New England if I had tried. I was passing through town today, and I saw a hundred stories in every face. I think he'll be pleased with what I come up with.''

She was interested. "So you'll be taking pictures of the townspeople, too? Not just the scenery?''

"Of course. That's the only way the book will ever talk. The camera can see things the human eye can't sometimes, restricted as we are by preconceived notions and prejudices and even our own sense of what is ordinary and what is extraordinary. A photograph can display a person's entire life story—which is why, I suppose, in the old days so much superstition was attached to photography. People used to believe that the photographer captured your soul on film, and that was what made the image. A lot of photographers were run out of town on a rail back then.''

Jennifer laughed. "Well, I don't think you're in any danger of that, but if you start taking pictures of people on Main Street, you're sure to stir up a lot of local curiosity. I thought you were protective of your privacy.''

Again he shrugged. "In a way, I still am. But I promised Jake this book, and it can't be done right without getting a little bit involved.''

Now she hesitated. She had asked it before and gotten no straight answer; she did not really expect one now. But it was the question that kept nagging her, begging for an answer; she could not ignore it any longer. "And, when you've taken your pictures and... and finished with New England... what then? Is Canada part of your assignment too?''

He captured a long strand of her hair between his thumb and forefinger, exploring its texture with a delicate rubbing motion, his eyes fixed in pleased fascination upon the halo of sheen formed by the firelight around her head. "No," he answered thoughtfully, "Canada was just another escapist ploy."

She tilted her face upward to look at him, puzzled. "Escape?"

His smile was somewhat absent, and he began to wind the strand of her hair about his finger with gentle absorption. "For the last six months," he said, "maybe longer than that, I've been running. That's why I took this assignment with Jake. To stay on the move, to keep on looking—for what, I don't know. I only know that the faster I ran, the farther away whatever I was looking for grew, and what I was running from only got closer."

"What were you running from, Adam?" she said softly, watching him, her eyes pleading with him to open up to her, ready to receive whatever he had to offer.

There was a softening of his face, a flicker of something in his eyes that was quickly subdued, and he said simply, "Myself, I guess. The truth you were talking about the other day that each of us has to find the courage to face eventually . . . all those basic things a man can't run away from because he carries them with him. And then . . ." As he wound her hair his hand had been drawn closer to her face; now it was resting against the side of her neck. He released the curled strand of hair and spread his warm fingers over the nape of her neck, cupping and shielding it, holding it with a loving presence. "One day in the midst of my frantic quest I stumbled upon fairyland and met a beautiful witch who granted my every wish. Strange things started happening to me, inexplicable things, good things. And the best part was that the road to this enchanted land only went one way; there is no exit. So here I stayed, and here I discovered that what I had been looking for all along was exactly the magic that I had stumbled upon by accident, in this enchanted place, under the spell of the beautiful witch." He smiled. "The end."

He had taken her breath away. Although the story was told lightly, its meaning was clear, and there was an unmistakable light of sincerity in his eyes. But how could she be sure of anything that came from this compelling stranger of a thousand contradictions... and how could she resist the pull he exerted on her heart?

In the end all she could say was a rather breathless, "You're a very esoteric person, aren't you? You should be a fantasy writer."

His hand moved away from her neck and rested casually on the sofa behind her, his lips tight with a slight, self-deprecating smile. "I don't have the time or the patience, and probably not the talent. I did write a children's book once, though, in college. I used it as a showcase for some experimental photography I was doing. The pictures were the only thing that sold it."

"Good heavens," Jennifer exclaimed softly. Her voice was a little tight and still somewhat breathless as she tried to pull herself out of the spell he had cast upon her only moments ago. His face looked so beautiful and vulnerable in the fire-light; she wanted to touch it with her hands and her lips, to breathe in the fragrance of him and taste his skin upon her tongue. The effect of his touch clung to her like a narcotic, and she wanted to feel his sinewy arms tighten about her; she wanted simply to be held by him. It was torture, sitting so close to him and not touching him, re-membering so clearly how it had been the last time they were together and trying desperately to follow his moods. "Is there no end to your talent? Photographer of lusty nudes, ace journalist, spin-ner of fairy tales par excellence.... I'm im-pressed."

He inclined his head majestically.

And then she inquired seriously, "Whatever made you lose interest in writing for children? You obviously have the talent."

"I consider that high praise indeed," he teased her, "coming from the world-renowned librarian." And then he answered her question. "There's more money in photography, for one thing, and I never had the patience to develop the skills it takes to write well, and, oh, a lot of reasons. I've often thought about giving it a try again, but I never had the time. Besides, after years spent as a photographer of lusty nudes and an ace journal-ist it's pretty hard to see through the eyes of a child again. Speaking of which," he declared sud-denly, rising, "I must propose a toast." He took the two glasses from the mantel, and she rose to accept hers. He smiled as he looked at her, the light in his eyes deepening with sincerity, and he said softly, "To the lady who made me see the magic."

Warm pleasure flowed through her like the nectar of the wine not yet tasted. She looked at him, and she had never known a more perfect moment in her life, a moment that lacked for nothing and was filled to overflowing, a moment in which all she had ever wanted was reflected in his eyes. He raised his glass; she followed suit. The clink of the two glasses echoed like a chime throughout the room.

His face was a misty glimpse of promise through the rich red veil of the wine in her glass. So easy, so beautiful. Deep red with a flicker of fire churning in its depths, fascinating, mesmerizing. She could not help looking at it, the way the light of the fire caught upon the crystal and was reflected like a candle in the red velvet liquid, a spark that jumped and twisted and cavorted with pleasure, blinking and shifting in tune with the pulsing of her heart. . . . She couldn't look away; she couldn't resist its allure. The flame that played in her glass had captured her just as surely as the elusive, enigmatic man who had poured the wine and was undoubtedly about to prove just as dangerous.

By the time the aura came it was too late. She felt it beginning in the tips of her fingers and sweeping upward, spreading, invading her, closing in on her, and sealing her into its shell. She heard the crash of the glass that slipped from fingers no longer able to grasp; she saw, or thought she saw, the reflected fragments of its shattered light dancing before her eyes. And then there was nothing, nothing but those blinking and dancing fragments of multicolored light....

Time passed. She always came back with a sense of time having passed, of having missed something, a great chunk of emptiness blocking the passage between what had gone before and what was now. It was not a pleasant process, this slow journey from the beyond into a cold and painful reality. The hollowness in her stomach weighted her down; her limbs were tied with cobwebs and devoid of sensation; her vision was misty and fragmented. Faraway voices echoed and blurred; there was a high, thin buzzing in her ears; and piece by piece, moment by moment, the world began to shift and turn and fit into place again.

She heard his voice saying her name, far away at first, tone and expression indistinguishable, then gradually becoming clearer. And then she felt the presence of him, his touch, his hands gently cupping her shoulders, the warmth of his chest near hers, the whisper of his breath across her face. "Jenny..." Adam's voice was soothing, comforting, calm and steady. She was dully aware that she had been expecting him to be shouting at her. Why wasn't he shouting? *Everyone always shouted....* "It's all right, love." *Soft, comforting.* "It's all right, I'm here...don't be afraid."

His voice fell over her like a warm blanket, soothing her like a caress. She was tired. So tired. Her muscles strained to hold up her weary body.

She could hardly keep her eyes open. She wanted to sink into the embrace of that calm, reassuring voice.

"What is it, Jenny?" Still calm, he seemed remarkably unafraid. "Tell me. Tell me what to do. What do you need?"

"Sleep," she managed thickly after a long time. "I need ... to sleep." Later she would think, later he would be angry with her, later there would be so much to regret and to hate, but now it was all she could do to force her legs to move within the supporting circle of his arm as he led her to the sofa. She did not feel it when her cheek touched the cushion.

Fifteen minutes later she opened her eyes. The lethargy was gone; she felt refreshed and well-rested. But that was only for a moment, and then she remembered.

She remembered, and despair began to close in on her in great smothering clouds. Everything had been so perfect....

Adam was standing by the window with his back to her, the muscles of his arms stretched taut as he leaned against the sill, looking out. Her heart turned and clenched with yearning and sorrow as she looked at him, wanting him, wanting to call back the last half hour and erase it from the memory of time.... Time. Wishing they had had more time. He wasn't ready to deal with this; she had no right to ask him to deal with this. What they had lost tasted like the salt of tears in the back of her throat.

She turned her head, looking bleakly up at the

ceiling. Bear, immediately sensitive to her slightest movement, came over to her with a small whine of concern in his throat; his master followed.

Jennifer took a breath and found her courage. She even managed to smile as she stroked Bear's head reassuringly, and in a moment she met Adam's eyes. They were dark with concern and confusion. "Well," she said. "Now you know my deep dark secret."

She could not meet his eyes for more than that moment; she was too afraid of what she might read there. She sat up, and he took her arm to support her. "Can I get you anything?" he asked. There was nothing more than tender concern in his voice, no accusation on his face.

"No." Her voice was a little weak, she strengthened it with another smile, which faded almost as soon as it began. Her eyes flickered across his face again, noting the worried line between his brows and the anxious lines near his mouth, and then she looked away. After a moment, twisting her hands together in her lap, she asked falteringly. "Was it—very long? Did I do anything or—or—"

"No," he assured her, sitting beside her. "It was only about three minutes. You just stared." As always, her relief at the answer to that question was as overwhelming as her compulsion to ask it. And then he said quietly, "It scared me, Jenny."

"Yes." For a moment that was all she could manage. But then she knew she could not avoid it any longer; he was waiting for an explanation. He had a right to know. She had to face it. She took another deep breath and reached for all her courage. Forcefully she unclasped her hands, and she met his eyes bravely. There was nothing to be ashamed of. She was *not* ashamed. "I have a minor form of epilepsy," she told him calmly. "What you just saw is called a petit-mal seizure. It's not dangerous. It's just... like a momentary short-circuit in the brain or something." He did not look shocked, or repelled. He simply nodded, waiting for her to go on. "I don't always know when it's going to happen," she went on. With a great effort she kept her eyes steady on his. She knew if she looked away from him, she would never be able to face him again. "A lot of things can trigger it. Something unexpected or sudden, like the accident in the truck... or something as simple as the way the light caught in the wineglass just now. It's blinking lights, usually, and bright colors, red and blue especially. The lights on police cars and fire engines."

Still he said nothing. He simply looked at her, and listened to her. Jennifer could not tell what he was thinking. She wanted desperately to know. She wondered if he had any idea how much it cost her to tell him this, how painful this confession was for her, wrapped as it was in so many years of superstition and fear and the reactions of outsiders to what was, after all, not so uncommon a condition.... She wondered if he guessed how much she feared his rejection and dreaded the look of caution and sympathy that would eventually cross his face, how desperately she had hoped he would never have to know, because she only wanted to be thought of as a normal woman by him. He could not know how desperately she had wanted everything to be right between them. And now she had lost it all; he would never see her in the same way again.

She had to go on. She couldn't just sit there with the silence carving its own wide chasm between them. She had to say something, even though nothing she could say would make a difference. "People used to think stress brought on the seizures," she said. "So everyone pampered me and treated me like an invalid as a child, and I really hated that, you know? And those who didn't smother me with attention always kind of kept their distance, trying not to look at me like I was a freak, as though they were afraid I was contagious.... Anyway, it's not stress. It's not emotional or psychological at all, it's a chemical-mechanical thing. It just happens, sometimes, and ..." Her voice was beginning to sound hollow even to her own ears. She couldn't go on any longer. She dropped her eyes. "I'm sorry you had to see it. I know it must have frightened you."

"It did," he admitted. "It was as though you had ... slipped away from me, and nothing I could do would bring you back. It was a helpless feeling." He hesitated. "How long have you had it?"

He was sitting very close to her, so that their arms brushed, and the heat from his body was comforting. So was the way he spoke, not condemning or judgmental, just matter-of-fact. Curiously accepting. It occurred to her that he was the first person she had ever met who had reacted so calmly to one of her seizures or to learning of her condition. She was enormously grateful for that. She wished he could know how much his quiet acceptance meant to her, how grateful she was to him for not revealing whatever emotions he must be experiencing now. His attitude made it so much easier for her.

She answered, "All my life. I was on medication—a tranquilizing drug—up until last year, and that kept the seizures under control somewhat. But then I realized that, well, it was like when I was having a seizure I might be missing maybe three or four minutes out of my life, and that wasn't pleasant—but while I was on those drugs I was missing *everything*. I wanted to try to live a normal life without them, and I've never regretted the decision. Everything is so much clearer now; it's almost as though since I've been off the medication I've learned to really see for the first time. I knew that without the drug I would be more prone to seizures and that they would be worse, but it was something I knew I would just have to live with. And I'm not sorry."

He was silent for a very long time. She did not look at him, once again afraid of what she would find in his eyes. But it didn't matter. She had told him; she should have told him long ago, for she had nothing to be ashamed of. He would either accept her as she was or reject her because of a medical problem she could not control, but either way there was no turning back from here. And she was not sorry. It had happened, it could not be undone, and now he knew. It was up to him.

He said quietly in a moment, "That must have taken a lot of courage."

She glanced at him. His face was very sober, and he was looking at his hands. There was no way to read what was in his eyes. "Not really," she answered. "I just decided to live the best I could under conditions I couldn't control." He still did not look up. She turned away and absently stroked the dog, who sat attentively at her feet. "I do live a completely normal life," she added, and she hoped he did not think she was pleading for him to believe her. On this subject she would not plead with anyone. "The only dangers are in operating heavy equipment or—or in driving; otherwise I mostly do whatever I want to."

He said nothing. He simply sat there looking down at his hands, and the lines on his face were very grave. She thought he did not know what to say. What could he say? Even her closest friends were still sometimes awkward when it came to dealing with her special problem, and he was a complete stranger. He had not asked to be burdened with this. She had no right to ask him to accept this. It had nothing to do with him; it wasn't his problem.

She said quietly, "I guess I'd better leave."

He looked up quickly. "Don't go."

She could not be certain whether the offer was made sincerely or out of mere politeness. She shook her head slowly, pulling on her boots. "No. It's late and, well, let's face it, the spirit of the evening is kind of shot now anyway."

"It's not late," he said firmly, standing beside her. "You don't have to leave."

"Look, I'm all right," she said tightly, trying desperately to push back her own emotions, which were tangling inside her like coiled springs. "I'm sorry it happened, and I appreciate your being so understanding, but you don't have to patronize me anymore. I'm fine and...I think I'd just better go."

"I'll walk you home."

She whirled at the door, and the despair she had been trying so valiantly to control burst through. "Do you see what I mean?" she cried. "You're doing it—fussing over me, patronizing me. I'm not an invalid! I'm not a china doll, and I don't need special care!"

"There's nothing patronizing about my wanting to walk you home," he returned shortly. "It's dark out and—"

"No." She did not think she could bear to be with him any longer, watching every moment for that look of sympathetic restraint to cross his face...knowing that he was only being kind to her because he felt sorry for her. She slipped on her coat and shook her head again firmly, not looking at him. "No."

He hesitated for a moment. And then, when she opened the door, he made a soft sound and commanded, "Bear. Go."

Immediately responsive, the dog wiggled out beside her and walked her all the way to her door. When she bent down to pet him, tears of sorrow and loss choking her throat, her eyes fell upon the house across the way. Adam was standing there, silhouetted in the light from the open door, watching her. Her throat clenched on another gulp of thick tears, and she suddenly knew that if she lifted her hand to him he would come. She wanted him to come to her at that moment more than anything in the world.

But she simply dismissed the dog, took out her key, turned, and went inside.

Chapter Seven

"Well, for goodness sake, Jenny, what did you expect?" Jo Ellen demanded patiently. "You must have scared the poor fellow half to death. You could hardly expect him to just go on and pretend nothing had happened. Of course he was upset. You know how people are.... And he's an outsider—he doesn't know you or love you like we all do—you couldn't expect him to understand."

Jennifer shrugged, picking the crust off her tuna sandwich. "That's not it. I mean, he was really very calm about the whole thing. It's just not a very good way to start a relationship."

Jo Ellen's eyes sharpened. *"Relationship?"* She lifted her eyebrows in quickened interest and sat back against the brown vinyl booth. "Things have gone that far, have they?"

Again Jennifer shrugged. They were having lunch at the drugstore during the busiest time of the day, and this was not the place she would have preferred to have this conversation. In fact, she would have preferred not to have this conversa-

tion at all. Her emotions were still too tangled, and
she was incapable of being objective. Only a long-
ingrained habit had persuaded her to confide in
her sister, and now she wished she had never
started it.

"I don't know, Jo." She sighed. "Everything is
so confusing. He's confusing. I just wish..." Her
voice trailed off, not exactly certain what she
wished.

Jo Ellen was thoughtful for a moment. "He
seemed very nice," she admitted. "He's certainly
had an interesting life. I always wondered what
kind of men did those nasty centerfolds, but he's
just like anyone else, isn't he? At least he seemed
so to me."

Jennifer's lips tightened with a repressed smile.
So, Jo Ellen *had* gotten his life story out of him;
Jennifer wasn't surprised. And Jennifer said softly, "Actually, he's not like anyone I've ever met
before in my life."

Jo Ellen watched her carefully, not missing the
softening of her face nor the faraway look in her
eyes. "Hmm," she murmured at last. "This is
more serious than I thought." Then she sat forward, the concerned big-sister look on her face.
"Honey, you know I don't like to interfere...."

Jennifer rolled her eyes in silent denial, and Jo
Ellen said defensively, "Well, I don't! I was just
going to say," she added patiently, "that he's just
a stranger passing through, and you really don't
know anything about him. Granted, he seems like
a nice young man, and I'm sure he'd be very
good-looking if he put on a little weight and got

some sun, but don't you think you should be careful? I mean, the two of you out there all alone...."

"Good heavens," complained Jennifer. "You make him sound like the Boston Strangler."

"No," replied Jo Ellen thoughtfully. "I was just wondering...do you suppose there's much money in doing centerfolds?"

"I don't think you're the type," returned Jennifer acidly, then drained her milk shake. And at Jo Ellen's indignant protest she explained patiently, "He's not doing centerfolds anymore; he's doing a perfectly respectable book on life in the United States. I don't know how much he's getting paid, and I don't care, but I'm sure he'd tell you if you asked him." And at Jo's thoughtful look she challenged, "Don't you dare." She crumpled her napkin and picked up her purse. "I'm going back to work before this conversation gets out of hand."

"Ask him to have Thanksgiving dinner with us," Jo Ellen suggested suddenly.

"So you can give him the third degree?" retorted Jennifer.

"Not at all," replied Jo Ellen innocently. "He's our tenant, and he has no family here, and it's only the decent thing to do."

Jennifer hesitated and slipped on her coat. Then, without looking at her sister, she said, "I doubt if I'll be seeing much of him anymore." It hurt to say that. "See you later, Jo," she added, and left quickly before her sister could trap her with more questions.

Jennifer tried not to be depressed as she finished out the workday. In fact, she tried not to think about Adam at all. Jo Ellen was right, of course—Jennifer knew nothing about him. It was foolish to care so much for him, to let herself get involved so deeply in such a short period of time. Why should she care what he thought of her, why should it bother her that what had happened last evening would come between them? He would be leaving at the end of the month, anyway....

It was late in the afternoon when Joseph Underwood came in. At first Jennifer was disoriented, because when the pleasant masculine voice said, "Hello, Jenny," she thought for one brief, heartstopping moment it might be Adam. She tried to hide her confusion and her disappointment as she returned his greeting, and then she felt a twinge of apprehension as she thought she suspected why he had come.

The last time they had seen each other seemed to belong to another lifetime. She could not believe it had been only two weeks ago. On that occasion this earnest young man had made her a proposition she had almost considered accepting, and he had promised he would ask her again. Jennifer knew now, intensely, she did not want him to ask her again.

But she smiled and tried not to look nervous as she said, "Back again so soon? I wouldn't have thought you'd had time to read all the books you took out last time."

He smiled. "Actually I haven't. I've come on another matter."

Oh, no, Jennifer thought in despair. But there was no way to avoid it. She would turn him down as gently as possible and try not to hurt his feelings. She hoped that he would not notice that although her answer was the same as it had been last time, her reasons for giving it had vastly altered.

But, typically of him, he did not jump straight into the subject. Instead he hedged with, "You're not looking quite your usual cheerful self this afternoon. Is anything wrong?"

Jennifer knew a sleepless night showed on her face—that was how Jo Ellen had dragged the story out of her in the first place—and it was hard to be cheerful when she was trying to direct all her energy toward keeping her heart from breaking. But she assured him, "Just desperately overworked. How are you?"

She noticed for the first time a sober cast to his face; she began to have second thoughts about his reason for coming here. "I'm never at my best when I have an unpleasant task to perform," he said. He hesitated, dropped his eyes, and then placed a book on the desk. "Jennifer," he said, "I need to talk to you about this."

It was a copy of *The Tale of Elias Cotton*. Upon closer examination she noticed it was the library copy. "I don't remember your checking this out," she said in surprise.

"I didn't." His tone was grim. "One of the members of my congregation—Mrs. Patten—did."

Jennifer should have known what was coming.

Mrs. Patten was a stern-nosed, frustrated, militant old busybody who received her greatest pleasure from causing trouble for other people. Jennifer had never had any personal dealings with her, but she knew her reputation well.

"She was...shocked," Joseph said carefully.

Jennifer got a picture of that particular lady with this particular book, and she tried not to giggle. "I can well imagine she would be."

Joseph took a breath. "Jennifer, she wants the book taken off the shelves."

Jennifer stared at him. "You can't be serious."

"I'm very much afraid I am." And if she had needed further proof, the tight, unhappy expression on his face would have convinced her.

Still, she could not believe it. "Look, if she doesn't want to read it, she doesn't have to, but that's no reason to keep everyone from reading it. That's ridiculous, Joseph!"

He looked very uncomfortable. "She considers this book a threat to the morality of the community," he confessed. "She insists that it be taken off the shelves."

Jennifer could not prevent a bark of astounded laughter. She quickly lowered her voice when heads turned in disapproving scowls toward her. "Come on, you can't mean..." And then she hesitated, an awful suspicion dawning on her. "Do you...do you agree with her?"

Jennifer thought she had never seen a more miserable visage in her life. "Jennifer, you've got to understand, as a minister it's my duty to protect my congregation, and as a representative of my church I'm obligated to do what I feel is best for the community."

She insisted, rather coldly, "Do you agree with her?"

"Yes," he said, meeting her eyes determinedly. "I do."

It took a moment for Jennifer to gather her thoughts and her temper and to subdue her incredulity. When she spoke, her voice was remarkably calm. "Have you read the book?" she inquired.

"Certain, er, passages," he admitted, and a very faint flush tinged his cheeks. "Which I found extremely offensive—"

"And which, I'm sure," retorted Jennifer acerbically, "you carefully underlined in red pencil so the next reader would be sure not to miss the 'good parts'!"

His color only deepened. "Now, Jennifer, it was nothing like that, and you know it. You yourself have a responsibility to the community—"

"I have a responsibility to provide quality reading material, and that is exactly what I do," interrupted Jennifer firmly. She really could't believe this. As far as she was concerned this ridiculous conversation had gone far enough. "And now, if you'll excuse me, I do have work to do." She looked at him pointedly. "Responsibilities to fulfill."

"Jennifer, I'm trying to do you a favor," he said lowly. Impatience tinged his voice. "After Mrs. Patten found this"—he gave the book on the counter a distasteful flick with his fingernail—"she came back and scoured your shelves.

Do you have any idea what kind of books she brought into my office?''

"It's beginning to sound as if she has too many outstanding books on her card," Jennifer said calmly. "I'll have to check into it."

"I'm talking about *The Catcher in the Rye, East of Eden, Tom Jones* . . . those are only a few of the classics she pulled. She wants to have them *all* recalled."

Now Jennifer was certain he couldn't be serious. "How did she miss *Madame Bovary*?" she inquired mildly.

"Jennifer," he said soberly, "if you'll work with me on *The Tale of Elias Cotton,* I'm sure I can convince her to forget about the other books. But if not . . ."

"If not, we'll have the emptiest library in the States," responded Jennifer dryly. "I know. Really, Joseph, you can't expect me to take this seriously. Give me credit for a little intelligence, will you? This is all just one person's opinion; she can't dictate the reading habits of the rest of the community."

"She's planning to take this to the library committee," he assured her gravely. "And if you and I can't reach some sort of agreement on this, I'm afraid I'm going to have to back her. Please think about it, Jennifer," was his final request before he turned and left.

For a long time Jennifer simply stared after him. The whole thing was still too incredible to be alarming, but mostly she was disappointed in Joseph. He was educated, well-read, much too intelligent to fall for this kind of ploy for attention.... Yet for all intents and purposes he was letting himself be used by one narrow-minded old lady in a crazed quest that practically reeked of book-burning. She had sadly misjudged him, and that realization only added to her depression.

Someone placed a stack of books on the desk, and she turned automatically to check them. "Your card, please?"

"I'm sorry, I don't have one."

She looked up, her heart giving one unpreventable little lurch at the sound of the familiar voice before it began to pump with a slightly escalated rhythm again. "A-Adam," she stammered. "I—I didn't see you come in."

"You were rather involved." He nodded toward the door by which Joseph had just left, frowning a little. "What was that all about? You seem upset."

She hesitated, looking at him, distracted and disoriented. He was wearing a white sweater over an open-throated pale blue shirt and gray slacks; he looked well groomed and healthy and, to her, incredibly handsome. His thick blond hair was shiny and fluffy, and the sun's glow had tinted his cheeks a very pale brown. She had only to look at him to be filled with yearning and wonder, and for a moment she forgot the question, forgot to answer, and she thought nothing except that he was here, felt nothing except the surprised, anxious thumping of her heart.

Then he prompted, "Or isn't it any of my business?"

"Oh.... Oh, no," she managed. She tried to still the nervous pounding of her pulses. What was he doing here? He was acting so normal, so casual, just as though nothing had happened.... Why? What was he thinking? "No," she explained, "that was just the local minister on a proxy intimidation mission. It seems one of his parishioners has found something objectionable about the sort of reading material I provide. She wants to take *Elias Cotton* off the shelves."

The disturbed frown deepened. "What are you going to do?"

But her mind was no longer on *Elias Cotton,* Mrs. Patten, or Joseph Underwood. That was the least of her concerns right now. "Oh, nothing," she replied distractedly. "They'll forget all about it in a few days." What she really wanted to know was why he had come, what his being here meant, what he expected her to say to him now, or whether he had something to say to her....

"I don't know, Jenny," he said thoughtfully, "this sort of thing has been happening in small communities around the country for the past few years. You'd be surprised how much trouble a group of outraged citizens can cause an innocent librarian. Be careful how you handle them."

"I'm not worried," she said, yet something tightened within her at his concern. It was something wonderful and warm that superseded even her present uncertainties, and when he smiled at her a warm glow spread throughout her body.

"No," he said gently. "I guess you're not.

There isn't too much that frightens you, is there, Jennifer?''

She turned quickly to begin typing up his library card. She did not want him to see the expression on her face because he would surely realize that the one thing that frightened her now was losing him. "I'm afraid of a lot of things," she replied, "but I try not to borrow trouble from the future. I'll just make you up a temporary card and you can use it any time you want while you're here...." She finished typing his name and address, trying to keep her smile casual as she turned back to him. "Planning to spend the evening reading?" she inquired lightly, eyeing the large stack of books.

"Not tonight," he answered. "Tonight I thought you and I could go out to dinner. I noticed a place on the highway this afternoon that looked nice, and if you don't mind leaving now, we'll get an early start on the evening. It's about fifteen miles out."

She could not keep her surprise from showing in her eyes. What was it, a gesture of sympathy toward her? An attempt to prove something to her? Just a friendly invitation to repay her for all her attention while he had been ill? Though she knew it was exactly the wrong thing to say, she couldn't help it. "Why?" she asked.

A mixture of puzzlement and amusement lightened his eyes. "Well, it seems to me I owe you dessert from last night, and since I finished off the pie for breakfast ..." His brow creased curiously.

"What do you mean, *why*? What kind of question is that?"

Jennifer did not believe in avoiding the issue. She took a breath and said calmly, "Look, Adam, you don't have to be nice to me. I appreciate the effort, but it's just not necessary."

He seemed genuinely confused. "It is if I want it to be. What are you talking about? Why are you acting so strange?"

She dropped her eyes, hoping she had misjudged him, knowing only one way to find out for sure. "I just . . . didn't expect to see you again after last night, that's all," she said quietly.

There was a silence, a very ominous one, and she had to look up. His frown now was no longer confused; it was dark and unpleasant. He said in a low tone, "I don't think I like what you're suggesting. Will you do whatever it is you have to do to my books and then get your coat so we can talk about this outside?"

Her heart began to thump erratically again, and she was not certain whether it was from dread or anticipation. She looked at him for a moment, almost starting to protest, but his expression was adamant. She turned uncertainly and asked her assistant to check his books and to lock up for her when she left, and by the time she retrieved her coat and her purse Adam was waiting for her at the door.

He placed the books in the backseat of the Blazer and helped her inside, and when he slid behind the wheel he turned to her. "Look, Jennifer,'' he said gently, ''I know you have a right to be sensitive. I imagine you've grown up with a lot of censure and superstition and fear, and I imagine you've gotten some strange reactions from people when they learn about your condition. I don't know why that should be, unless people are just naturally afraid of what they don't understand. But, Jenny, please don't categorize me, okay? If I said or did anything last night to make you think I think less of you because of what you told me, I'm sorry. I didn't mean to.'' He smiled at her tenderly, and the light that grew in his eyes as they swept her face was almost wondering. ''You are a very, very special person,'' he said softly. ''Everything I learn about you only makes you more unique. Please don't pull away from me now.''

She was blushing, both with embarrassment at his direct confrontation of a subject that had, to her, always been wrapped in secrecy and distaste, and with pleasure at the warm emotions his acceptance drew from her. She loved him. The knowledge filled her with a quiet, unshakable certainty, and warmed every part of her. She did not want to pull away from him. She only wanted to get close to him, to let him fill her life as her love for him filled her soul. And she wanted it for a long, long time.

When she smiled at him, hesitantly yet reassuringly, his finger touched her chin lightly, tracing the birthmark. In his eyes for just that moment she thought she saw a reflection of all she was feeling—the warmth, the adoration, the need—and just as her own emotions quickened in wondering response he turned away and started the engine.

In a moment he said, "You'll have to forgive me if I ask some dumb questions, and if it embarrasses you or makes you uncomfortable to talk about it, I'll understand, but I really want to share this with you, Jenny. I know a little about petit-mal epilepsy from what I've picked up in my reading—just enough to guess that was what was happening during your seizure last night, but I don't really understand what it's all about." He glanced at her, interest and concern on his face. "Is it painful for you? Is there anything I should know, anything I should do . . . ?"

She shook her head, smiling a little, loving him. "No. There's nothing anyone can do to prevent it; it just happens. It's like I just . . . lose time; I don't feel anything or know anything—until it's over. Then I need to sleep for a few minutes, and I feel fine. The only thing that hurts," she added, almost to herself, "is the way people treat me afterward."

"It must have been hard for you," he said quietly.

"I suppose," she admitted after a moment. "It's just one of those things you learn to live with."

He was silent for a time. Then he said soberly, "I admire your courage, Jennifer. In fact, that's only one of the things I admire about you. You are the most extraordinary person I've ever met." Jennifer hardly thought she was deserving of such praise, and she looked at him in some confusion.

But he only smiled and reached for her hand, which lay upon the seat between them. When his fingers closed, warm and secure, about hers she forgot whatever it was she might have said in the softly flowing joy of just having him near.

The restaurant he had discovered was one Jennifer had never visited before, which was not surprising because she did not go out much. When she did go out it was usually to the locally approved places, and this restaurant was far beyond the budgets of any of the men she dated. It was an exclusive little inn fashioned after a Swiss chalet, set far off the road and featuring French cuisine, snow-white tablecloths, and heavy silver. It was obviously a tourist trap, and Jennifer told him so.

"So what?" he grinned. "I'm a tourist. Besides, when I'm on the road I eat at nothing but fast-food restaurants and cheap steak houses; I feel like treating myself."

"I wish you had told me," she whispered as they were seated, glancing around at the finely dressed men and women who shared the room, "so I could have dressed up."

"That would have spoiled the surprise," he scoffed. "Where's your spirit of adventure?"

She wanted to tell him that just being with him was adventure enough, but somehow she felt she didn't have to. It must have surely shone in her eyes. Jennifer had her first escargots—which were not as bad as she had expected—followed by a creamy asparagus soup and veal cordon bleu, and she enjoyed every morsel. The conversation that flowed between them was easy and natural, the candlelight and the muted music in the background creating a subtle atmosphere of romance that only enhanced the mood they shared. He wanted to know all about her background—what it was like to grow up in a small town—her sister, her parents, her college days, and in turn he told her about his childhood in the Midwest. He shared amusing anecdotes about his days as a centerfold photographer and some not-so-amusing ones about his time on the newspaper, and by the time they left the restaurant Jennifer felt as if she had known Adam forever. As a matter of fact, she realized with some surprise, she could hardly remember when he had not been a part of her life, and it was impossible to envision the time when he would not be there.

They drove home beneath one of the biggest, most brilliant moons she had ever seen, and its pearly white radiance seemed to weave a spell over the empty road and envelop the car and its two occupants in a gossamer shawl. When he pulled up in front of her house, she did not want to say good night, and she thought he did not, either, so she asked lightly, "Are you anxious to start devouring your book, or do you have time or a cup of coffee?"

He pretended thoughtfulness. "Well, now, given a choice between spending the evening with a good book and a beautiful woman..." He hesitated and then grinned at her. "I'll take the cup of coffee."

He built a fire while she put the coffee on, and when she came into the living room he caught both her hands and pulled her down beside him before the hearth. He looked at her for a moment thoughtfully, and that look made her heart race. She liked the way the firelight caught in his eyes and the way his expression softened when he looked at her. She wondered not for the first time what he was seeing that could transform his face into such tenderly assessive lines. And then he said, "What are all your friends and relatives and other sundry townsfolk going to say about your keeping company with the ill-reputed stranger in town?"

So he knew about small-town suspicions and gossip. She couldn't help laughing. "Oh, all sorts of nasty things, probably. Jo likes you, though. She invites you to have Thanksgiving dinner with us."

"Thanks," he replied. "I accept." His hand had been resting lightly atop hers; now it traveled upward to caress her sweater-clad arm. Still he looked at her as though he were memorizing her face. "Will you do me a favor?" he said.

"Of course." Her voice was a little breathless. It was impossible to keep a steady tone when he looked at her like that, his eyes so rich with promise.... She was half afraid to read too much into that promise, and yet excited anticipation clenched within her at his touch; she waited in suspended urgency for his next word, his next move.

"Take your boots off," he requested simply. "And"—his eyes traveled upward, skimming over her face, resting near her eyes—"will you take your hair down for me?"

Her throat was tight, and a ridiculous pulse pounded there as she bent to remove her boots. The warm color in her cheeks was caused by nothing more than the way he looked at her as she reached up slowly and pulled the pins from the tight knot in which she had bound her hair. His eyes widened and lightened with pleasure as she shook the golden red halo free about her shoulders; on a compulsion he reached forward and cupped a handful of its shimmering essence in his fingers.

"You are so beautiful," he said softly.

Jennifer thought of her plain little body, completely devoid of alluring feminine curves, with its coltish limbs and pixie face and utterly dull features, and honesty compelled her to shake her head. She lowered her eyes shyly. "You know that's not true. You've seen—and photographed— some of the most beautiful women in the world; I don't even begin to compare."

"Jenny." Both of his hands moved to cup her face, tilting it upward; his eyes were wide with wonder and deep with sincerity. "How can you think about comparing yourself with any of those women? You are one of a kind, an original, and that's what makes you beautiful. That incredible hair. . . ." He threaded his fingers through it at the temples, and his eyes traveled over her face in slow, appreciative delight. "Those funny golden eyes that see so clearly things normal people don't. . . ." His fingertip brushed over her lashes, and she caught her breath. "That cute little nose, the perfect mouth. . . ." His finger traced a pattern there, slow and tingling, and her lips trembled, aching for the touch of his mouth. Every word he spoke drew her deeper into the spell cast by his eyes; every touch of his fingertips sent new quivers of electric anticipation through her. "The mark of an angel on your chin sets you apart from every other woman in the world...special, chosen..." His fingers feathered over the column of her throat; she thought he surely must notice the wild pulse that beat there. "Your lovely long neck, your slender shoulders...." His voice grew husky as his eyes, and his hand, lowered. "Your small, perfect breasts...." Discovering her by touch, his hands moved over her breasts, tracing their shape, sliding downward to her waist. He seemed almost to be speaking to himself, and her heart resounded against her rib cage, all but blocking out his voice. She struggled to keep her breathing even, and the rise and fall of her chest strained against his palms. "Your tiny waist, just the size of my hands, your slender hips...." His hand moved downward over the curve of her hip and her thigh, resting upon her calf, then slowly upward again beneath her skirt, over her knee. "Your long, lovely legs...." His voice was hoarse, his eyes dark yet at the same time bright enough to blind. Jennifer could no longer maintain her attempt to disguise what his touch was doing to her breathing as his hand moved upward over her stocking-covered thigh, stroking and caressing, awakening her senses with feathery touches that felt like electrical sparks. "Jenny, every time I'm near you I want to touch you, I want to feel every part of you, I want to undress you and discover you and I want to make love to you, Jenny...."

"Adam." The word was but a feathery whisper as his lips fell upon her throat, a gentle clasp that was nonetheless invasive; it shook her to the core of her deeply restrained yearning and sent a fever flaming through her that actually, for a moment, made everything throb brightly. His fingers tightened and circled about her thigh; she arched her neck to the slow burning course of his lips until their mouths met in desperate urgency. She clung to him, pressing herself closer even as his hand left her thigh and moved to the small of her back, tightening and drawing her into the circle of his legs, lowering her to the floor, pulling her closer. His warmth engulfed her and fed her forever; his leg tightened about hers and pressed her into the hardness of his pelvis, his chest straining against hers and his mouth bruising hers but meeting nothing but the overwhelming power of his own passion in response. There was a desperation to his kiss, and there was an urgency in hers, each of them seeking to draw from the moment all that they could, as though fearing it would soon be snatched away. Jennifer couldn't get close enough to him, she could not have enough of him, she wanted only to be a part of him in every way that was possible....

He dragged his mouth away from hers, to trace her face roughly, and his arms did not lessen their hold. His breathing was hot and uneven against her ear; she could feel the jerk of his heart against hers and the broken rise and fall of his chest.

"Oh, God, Jenny," he whispered raggedly. "I love you so much!"

For a moment everything within her was suspended, rapt, echoing and reechoing with the dazzling import of his words. Her breath was choked off in her throat; even her heart forgot to beat. And then his embrace gentled somewhat, his lips closed lightly upon her temple, and he whispered, "Yes. I said it, and I'm not sorry. I don't think I could have gone another day without telling you." He turned her gently so that she lay upon the floor, his hand cushioning her head, his other arm encircling her waist. In his eyes was something so beautiful it brought tears to hers; in his eyes was all she had ever wanted and never dared to hope for—the wonder of love, the power of joy. "The moment we met," he said softly, "the shock of touching you was just a reflection of what went on inside me ... if it wasn't love at first sight, it was the closest anyone can ever come." His hand moved from her waist to her face, and his eyes dropped to follow the path his fingers traced along the curve of her jaw. There was an unsteadiness to his touch, as though of emotions carefully contained, a warmth and a gentleness that felt like feather kisses.

"I tried to deny it at first; I couldn't believe what was happening," he went on in a soberer tone. "I thought if I ignored it, it would go away—things like that only happen to fools and kids, and I had no intention of getting involved. And then, when I left you, I really was leaving—but only with my body. My mind and my heart were still back here with a red-haired girl who simply wouldn't leave me alone." He looked at her, and his fingers fell still against her face. His eyes were very deep, his tone solemn. "I never intended to come back, Jenny. You've got to understand, I couldn't come back. But whatever it was—fate, or a wrong turn, or just my subconscious mind telling me where I really wanted to be—I found myself back here, and I knew it couldn't escape from you. It made me angry, because I knew it was wrong, that nothing could come of it but pain, but I didn't seem to have control...."

His eyes lowered, resting on her lips, her chin, downward to the rapid, erratic rise of her breasts.

"And then," he went on quietly, "the more I knew of you, the more I discovered that what I thought was only a schoolboy's imagination was real. And love at second sight was even better. Your courage, your intelligence, your insight, your determination, and your wisdom... You've changed my life, Jenny. You've made me see things I never dreamed of before; you've given me part of yourself, and it's something I'll never lose, and every time I'm around you, I only want more from you. I forget all the reasons I should leave you, and I just want to be selfish.... I want to pretend it can last forever...."

Her hand was trembling as it touched the taut muscle of his shoulder, curved around the back of his neck. She whispered, "I love you too, Adam." And the light that leaped from his eyes engulfed her as surely as his tightening arms and his seeking mouth. It was a kiss of urgent discovery and release, of boundless joy and growing need, and he broke away too soon. "Jenny." His whisper was ragged, the hand that stroked her cheek hot and unsteady. "Jenny, I want you, but..." His eyes searched hers anxiously, as though unable to believe what he saw there.

"Yes," she whispered. Her heart was thundering so powerfully it was an effort to form the word. But she meant it; with all her heart she wanted him. For whatever tomorrow might bring, he would belong to her tonight. This was their moment....

Still, in loving tenderness, he insisted, "Oh, love, are you sure? Is this right for you?"

Of that one thing she was sure. "More than anything," she whispered, and urged his face back to hers again.

He looked at her for a long time, memorizing and absorbing her features, and Jennifer, too, let herself be drawn into timelessness, committing to eternal memory the look in his eyes, this sharing of their hearts a prelude to the sharing of their bodies. And then, very gently, with utmost tenderness, he lowered his face to hers, simply resting against her and feeling the closeness for a moment. He wanted, as she wanted, to make the night last forever.

His lips moved over her face, slowly, tasting and adoring every inch of her with gentle deliberation, closing her eyes, brushing her nose, moving across her forehead and pressing into her temples, lingering for a long time on her chin, as though the mark there held a particularly wonderful fascination for him. And she returned his kisses, moving her face with his to taste the texture of his skin and to explore each sharp angle and each smooth plane, the silky substance of his eyebrow and the stubble of his lashes, the roughness of his shaven cheek and the incredibly soft fullness of his lips. She could feel the increased pace of his heart within the circle of her arms, and when his lips moved to her throat his warm hands slipped automatically beneath her sweater, tugging it upward. Melting instinctively, she lifted her arms and let him pull the garment over her head. For another long moment he simply looked at her, one hand resting upon the fragile swell of her rib cage, his eyes deep with pleasure and crystal clear with wonder. Jennifer was not ashamed to have him look at her: He saw something beautiful in her; he looked at her, and in his eyes was a reflection of something she had never seen before. She felt the warmth of the firelight playing upon her skin and the warmth of his adoration falling over her and the sensation was intoxicating. But when, with a short, soft breath he moved toward her again, she stopped him with a hand lightly upon his chest.

"Adam," she requested shyly. "Please, you too." She needed to see him as he had seen her, to feel his bared skin against hers, to make the exploration mutual. Without hesitation he understood, and slipped his own sweater over his head. And again understanding her needs without words, he let her unbutton his shirt and slowly push the garment from his shoulders.

With trembling wonder her hands moved over

the curve of his shoulders, cupping and caressing, down the smooth, tight muscles of his upper arms and across to his torso. Her fingers explored with delicate tactile sensitivity the muscles of his chest, the smoothness of his skin. She loved the way the muscles of his abdomen tightened when she touched him there and the way he caught his breath when her fingers paused over his dark brown nipples because she knew she was giving him pleasure. She wanted to give him pleasure; she wanted to know more of him, and she moved to taste with her lips and her tongue the texture of his skin as it glowed golden in the firelight. She could feel the spurred impetus of his breathing and taste the salt of a thin sheen of perspiration as her lips moved over his chest, and his responses filled her with a new and heady sense of joy. The hands that moved over her arms were light and unsteady until at last, with a soft groan, he drew her to him, lowering her to the carpet until their chests were molded against each other, flesh against flesh, the beat of one heart controlling the other.

His hands sought her breasts; she lost her breath as his mouth warmly covered hers and as his hands cupped and caressed, his fingers exploring and teasing her hardened nipples to a throbbing awareness. Then he lowered his face, his lips trailing over her throat and collarbone and down the center of her chest until his mouth closed over her breast. Everything within Jennifer tightened to focus upon the wonderful throb of sensation created by the play of his lips and his warm, moist tongue over her breast; concentrated awareness grew from the gentle sucking and probing motion of his mouth to a coiled ache within her abdomen that begged to expand. Her hands cupped his head, and unsteady fingers gathered silky handfuls of his hair. Her breathing had become nothing more than a series of erratic, shallow gasps, and her heart pumped fire through her veins. Through the veil of golden dizziness she was not aware of her soft moan of pleasure and urgency until his mouth came up to cover hers again, initiating a long, slow mating of lips and tongues that only tightened the need within her to an almost unbearable ache.

His hand moved to the clasp of her skirt as her own hands urgently explored the sensitive flesh around his waist. In movements natural and instinctive the last of their clothes were discarded and they lay at last in full body contact, holding one another, feeling the wonder of each part of undiscovered flesh as they molded themselves against each other. She could feel the thump of his heart and the heat of his face as it moved slowly against hers, the smoothness of his back muscles and the hardness of his buttocks her trembling fingers discovered, and she loved all that she knew. His hot breath fanned her face, and his loving lips touched her chin and her collarbone and her throat; his fingers were strong and smooth as they traced the curve of her hip and the indentation of her waist. And then his hand moved around and downward, and she knew nothing except the suspended wonder, the aching awareness, the intensely rapturous need that was generated from the knowing, exquisitely gentle exploration of his fingers.

The moment of the entry of his body into hers was prolonged forever, a moment frozen from eternity, the slow opening of a door that led them both into another world. And then they lay still for a time, holding each other in tight wonder and immeasurable joy, savoring the moment of their complete union with reverence and wonder, letting their love flow through them and between them to promise them forever.

But that was only the first step of the journey, and when at last Jennifer lay wrapped in the circle of his arms and legs and pressed into the slow, steady thumping of his heart, she was peaceful with the knowledge that they had shared something no amount of time could take away from them, and nothing could sever the cord of love that bound them. The last thing of which she was conscious before slipping into the compelling golden glow of sleep was his whispered words, "I love you, Jenny."

She closed her eyes and was content.

Chapter Eight

Jennifer was dreaming that she and Adam walked hand and hand in the snow. She dreamed of skating on the lake with her arm entwined with Adam's, and they were laughing. She dreamed the two of them stood at a frosty window while Christmas carolers sang outside; she heard the music. She dreamed she turned to place an ornament on the Christmas tree and that he kissed her under the mistletoe. And she saw her lovely warm dreams dispersed like dust on the wind when she opened her eyes and saw the pain and despair on Adam's face.

At some point he had covered them both with the afghan from the sofa, and his body was still warm next to hers, but the fire had died down to a mere glow, and when she looked at him she felt a chill. She did not know what had put that agony in his eyes; she did not know what—after all they had just shared—he could have found to come between them. But she knew it was real. And she knew that it came from the deep secret part of him he had been hiding from her all along, and that frightened her. But she tried not to let it show in her face or her voice; she fought away her own hurt and despair, and she placed her fingers lightly upon his lips.

"I'm not sorry," she said quietly before he could speak. "I don't regret anything, and I never will. If there was nothing more than this night, it would be enough to treasure for a lifetime. Please, don't say you're sorry."

He looked at her, and his pain was almost too much to bear. He turned his head slowly to look at the ceiling, and he whispered, "Oh, Jenny. I should be, but I'm not. And I hate myself for it." The lines about his mouth tightened, though still his voice remained soft. "And what about later? What about when I leave? Will it be enough for you then ... will it be enough for me? We never should have let this happen. It's only going to make it harder."

Why did he speak of leaving when she knew how much he loved her, when he knew she loved him? What could it be that called him away, and why wouldn't he tell her? She wanted to shout the questions to him; she wanted to drag an answer from him with her hands if necessary, but her instinctive response to his mood overwhelmed her own needs. Whatever it was, it was torturing him as much as it was her, and she would proceed gently, because she loved him.

"This is not the end for us, Adam," she said softly. "You're not leaving tomorrow. We have days, or weeks, however much time you can give me...."

"I should," he said bleakly. "I should leave now, today." And suddenly despair hardened his tone. He sat up. "God, Jennifer, you deserve more than this. You deserve a man who can offer you marriage, a home, children...." The sorrow in his eyes tore at her soul. "I wanted to be that man, Jenny...but I can't," he said harshly.

Her heart was slamming against her chest, her breath choking in her throat. She touched his arm, but he pulled away. He stood and began to pull on his pants.

She had to close her eyes against a sudden weakness and a seeping cold. She could not bear to watch him dress to leave her. Yet when she had given him her love tonight, hadn't she also given him her silent promise to let him go when the time came? No matter the reason for it, no matter if she must spend the rest of her life in yearning and confusion, she had traded it all for one eternal moment of perfect love. If she regretted the bargain, she must not let him know....

Jennifer took a breath; she made herself open her eyes. He had walked over to the window and parted the curtains and now looked out into the night, silently, hopelessly. She tried not to shiver, but the chill of loss was working its way from the center of her heart outward; she couldn't help it.

He said quietly, almost viciously, "How can you be so good? You've never asked me, never pressured me.... You knew I was keeping something from you, and you didn't force me—"

"I couldn't," she managed. Her voice sounded

weak, choking, racked with shivers. The afghan was lying on the floor near her, and she pulled it over her nakedness with clumsy, shaking fingers. She could feel it in the air, this terrible thing that was coming between them, and she wondered if the real reason she had never pried into his secrets was less her desire to respect his privacy than the fact that she really did not want to know.... Even now dread coiled within her, and she wanted to fight what he was about to say; she didn't want to admit anything bad into the treasured world they had formed. She could not let anything threaten what they had shared.

He said, still without looking at her, "Even now, when you have every right to know, when I owe you an explanation...." His harshly released breath was short and unsteady, the muscles on the back of his neck strained. And he added simply, "I can't do this tonight." He crossed the room suddenly; he pulled on his jacket. There was a low ferocity to his voice, an almost courageous determination. "Not to you, not to me."

She sat there, shivering and hugging the thin afghan to her, catching her breath between her teeth, and it took all her courage to refrain from calling out to him, to keep the sob from breaking through. At the door he paused, but he did not look back, as though he knew the look on her face would keep him there. "Tomorrow, Jenny." His half whisper was tight and broken. "I'll talk to you tomorrow."

And then she was alone.

Jennifer did not try to sleep that night. She dressed and sat by the fire and tried to keep from looking out the window where she knew she would see the lights burning in the house next door. She had never known such agony of the soul as she knew that night. If only she could have understood what was torturing him, what he was so determined to use to keep them apart, she thought she could have borne it. She could bear anything but this confusion, this tumultuous uncertainty, the pain of realizing that though he might love her, he did not trust her enough to share the deepest part of himself with her.

Perhaps he was right, perhaps the love they had shared had been a mistake, perhaps it would only make it harder, and perhaps it would not be enough.... But no. She had said it, and she meant it. She would never regret that one night of perfect love, the only love she had ever known.... Even if it never came again, it was hers, and nothing and no one could take it from her. It would be enough, if it had to be.

Only two things sustained her. He had promised he would talk to her tomorrow—*today*—she thought as she wearily pulled on her clothes and prepared for work. And she knew instinctively it was a promise he would not break. Adam loved her. She could not doubt that. He loved her as much as she loved him, and whatever must be faced, they could do it together. Surely whatever was frightening him so would pale in the light of their love....

By noon Jennifer realized she could not possibly
work a full day. She couldn't stay here, not knowing what was happening to him, not knowing what
might be waiting for her when she got home. . . .
In the cold light of day sweet eternal memories
began to fail and in their place came perfectly pre-
dictable and terrifying doubts. He could leave. He
could leave without saying good-bye, and she
would never see him again. What did a promise
mean from a man she hardly knew? What did his
love mean when he did not even trust her enough
to tell her why he could not stay? She would not
let him do that to her; she would not let him de-
stroy the miracle they had discovered together. . . .
She would not let him go without a fight.

　　She was just pulling on her coat and telling her
assistant to lock up for her when Rosemary
Adams came in, shivering dramatically and making elaborate shivering noises. "My, it's nasty out
there!" she exclaimed. "Looks like snow, if you
ask me."

　　She turned the collar of her coat down from her
rosy cheeks and greeted Jennifer with a bright
smile. "I thought I'd return these books on my
lunch hour," she said, placing a stack on the
counter. "On time for a change! Are you leaving,
dear? Not feeling well?"

　　Jennifer smiled and hoped to hide her pallor
and her swollen eyes from this astute lady. Rosemary Adams was Dr. Thompson's nurse, and if
she got the slightest hint that something was
amiss, she would report directly to the good doctor without hesitation. "No, nothing like that,"

replied Jennifer airily. "Just some personal business to take care of. How've you been, Rosemary?"

Rosemary began an enthusiastic account of her daughter's new baby, and Jennifer tried to look interested while keeping a discreet eye on the clock. Why did every minute suddenly seem so crucial? Why was this dread urgency building within her?

And then Rosemary said slyly, "And how is our handsome young patient doing these days?"

For just a moment Jennifer was taken aback, paranoically wondering if the sharp-eyed woman had read her thoughts. "Why," she managed, almost casually, "much better, I believe." The understanding smile in the other woman's eyes told Jennifer that her attempts to be nonchalant were ineffective. Adam had been right when he observed yesterday—had it only been yesterday?—that everyone in town would soon be talking about her keeping company with the "stranger."

"Well, if you see him," said Rosemary with a meaningful smile that changed the *if* to *when,* "do tell him that Doctor has received his records from Chicago and would like him to come in as soon as possible. You'll save me a trip out to the lake. Why doesn't the man have a telephone installed, I wonder?"

"He likes his privacy," Jennifer answered somewhat absently, for her mind had seized with some alarm on the message she had been asked to deliver. Why would Dr. Thompson want to see Adam again? He was recovered, wasn't he?

Rosemary's quick eyes sharpened in disapproval. "That's a very foolish attitude," she announced without qualification, "for someone in his condition. He should never be more than twenty minutes away from emergency medical treatment, and he knows that very well. No telephone indeed!" And then she paused, a look of genuine sorrow coming over her face. "It's such a tragedy, isn't it?" she said softly. "Cancer at his age.... His whole life ahead of him, and nothing can be done to help him. He does seem to be handling it well, though, don't you think? I was most impressed...."

Jennifer heard very little after the word *cancer*. The rest of Rosemary's speech faded into buzzing echoes of loosely connected logic, and there followed a period of shocked nothingness during which only that one word pounded over and over into her head: *Cancer*.

She must have said it out loud, because suddenly Rosemary stopped, a look of stunned dread coming over her face. "Oh, dear," she said weakly. "Did I say something out of place? Jennifer...I thought you knew. Please tell me you knew!"

Jennifer said nothing, and her mind was whirling and lurching and trying to absorb the rapidity with which all the pieces began to fall into place. *Cancer*. Adam was dying. That was the fear that drove him; that was the pain that tortured him; that was the secret he guarded so desperately.... But why? Why hadn't he told her? *Why?*

"Oh, Jennifer, I'm so sorry." Rosemary's

cheeks were white with consternation. "You know how Doctor feels about patient confidentiality.... If he ever found out that I'd been talking out of turn...Oh, I could just kick myself!"

Somehow Jennifer managed a very weak, very strained smile. "It's all right," she assured the nurse. "He'll never find out. You didn't do anything wrong."

But Rosemary did not look very reassured as she left the library.

Jennifer met Adam as she was coming out of the library. The air was bitter cold, and the sky was the exact color of his eyes—heavy, leaden, bleakly unrelenting. For a moment they simply looked at each other.

The hurt, the confusion, the shock, and the fear slowly drained away as she looked at him and saw only the man she loved. She said quietly, "I'm surprised you're still here."

"I would never leave without saying good-bye, Jenny," he said soberly. "I couldn't do that."

She simply nodded, not breaking the eye contact. "Give me a ride home?" she requested softly.

They did not talk on the way home, and he followed her inside without having to be asked. His face was drawn and his eyes bloodshot with sleeplessness, and she wondered, vaguely, if he intended to keep his promise and tell her the truth today. She saved him the trouble by turning to him and saying simply, "Dr. Thompson has your medical records. He wants to see you."

He looked at her for a very long time, and he

must have read it in her face. How could he not? Everything within her was torn and bleeding, and when the shock wore off the agony would begin. But for now all that registered in her face was the truth. The final truth. He said dully, "So. You know." His eyes were blank as he looked at her. "I'm glad."

She managed quite calmly, "When were you going to tell me?"

His long, slow breath reached her across the gulf of confusion that separated them, and it was as though in that breath he expelled a burden of tension and pain, secrets too long kept, silence gratefully broken. At last he looked at her, and on his face was only weary regret. "I know I should have told you sooner. I should have told you after the accident.... Instead I swore Dr. Thompson to secrecy."

"He didn't tell me," Jennifer felt for some reason compelled to reassure him, but it was as though he hardly heard. It didn't matter.

"You had a right to know what you were getting when you offered yourself to me last night," he continued in an oddly expressionless voice, not looking at her. "I had plenty of opportunities to tell you.... I almost did, several times. But always anger kept getting in the way, or pride. More than anything I was afraid of your pity."

"That's funny," she said softly, and her voice seemed to come to her from far away. "That's what I was most afraid of from you—pity."

There was a leap of recognition in his eyes, an empathy and the sharing of a single emotion, but it was gone almost before it registered. They both knew this was not the same thing. Not at all. She did not know how she made herself speak; she did not know how she could look at him so calmly and feel the demand to have it put into words. She did know that her legs could not support her any longer, and she had to sit down. She demanded of him evenly, "Tell me . . . everything."

Now that the time had come, all of the fight seemed to have gone out of him. Adam merely shook his head slowly, as though in wonder that he felt so little emotion over it, and he said simply, "It's such a long story; I'm not sure I know where to begin." But he would begin; he would tell her. He drew in a light, shallow breath and released it at leisure. "It began, I guess, a few years ago, when we decided—my wife and I—to start a family." A vague look came over his face, and his tone dropped a fraction, so he seemed almost to muse. "Or maybe it began long before . . . back in Vietnam. I don't know." Recovering himself abruptly, he seemed to dismiss it with a lift of his shoulder, and he looked back at her. "Anyway, when she couldn't get pregnant, we both went in for checkups, and that was just the beginning of so many tests and examinations; it seems as though the last two years of my life have been spent in hospitals. . . . I don't know whether the divorce was because of my sterility, or because I wouldn't fight back, or because . . ." Again that bleakness crossed his face. "She was just scared. Leukemia wasn't diagnosed until she had already started divorce proceedings, and she never knew." So many things, so many shocks, were bombarding her that Jennifer did not know why she seized on one particular thing to question him about. Perhaps it was because that one thing seemed the safest. "I—I don't understand," she managed. "Fight back? What did she expect you to do?" And already mixed anger and disgust were churning for the woman she did not know, the one who had deserted Adam in his time of need.

He responded briefly, "She wanted me to sue the government." And at Jennifer's confused look he explained wearily, "In Vietnam, I spent a lot of time photographing the aftermath of battles. Most air strikes were held in places that had previously been defoliated, because the jungle growth made it almost impossible to sight a target. The defoliant used was, of course, Dioxin. Agent Orange."

Jennifer felt the catch of her breath. She even heard the weak, reedy sound of her own voice. "Oh...God." But it was not until Adam looked at her that she realized the full significance of what he had revealed. He looked so calm, so accepting, so detached. It was perhaps the strength she sensed within him that kept her at that moment from going into hysterics.

He continued quietly, "I don't know, maybe she felt that taking some action would give her power over a situation she couldn't control... maybe it would have given her the same sort of satisfaction people get from revenge." He lifted his shoulders. "I never saw the point in it. Accusations and lawsuits wouldn't change anything; no one could prove that what happened to me wouldn't have happened with or without Dioxin.... But it became a crusade with her. There were citizens' action groups pressuring me, lawyers, doctors ready to testify... but I couldn't join the Hate Brigade. Enough damage had been done. Meanwhile my wife was dealing with it in her own way.... There were other men, there was a breakup... and neither of us knew then how bad it could get.''

He took another breath. "There was so much anger, so much hurt. My whole life was caving in at once. The divorce was final; she left town with some man, and a week later I was hospitalized and leukemia was diagnosed.''

There was a long, long silence. It was a silence of final acceptance, of adjustments made to things too deep and all-inclusive to be comprehended at once by the human mind. It was a time in which spirits were touched and changed forever.

And the remainder was almost an afterthought. "I've been in remission for six months,'' he said. "That's good, I suppose.... It's more of a chance than most people get. But I know that any day, any second...'' He looked at her, very quietly, very soberly. He was not afraid, just honest. "There is no cure, Jenny,'' he said simply. "My condition is stable but not improving. I was warned from the beginning not to cling to false hope, and this... second look at life I came here to take has helped me to accept the truth. Your courage has helped me. Please, don't let that courage fail me now," he finished, and his words were almost a whisper.

Was it courage that sustained her? Could it really be called heroism when she had no choice? No, it wasn't being brave when she had nothing left to lose. It wasn't courageous to watch the world shift and change and to adjust as best she could to a life that would never be the same. It was simply doing what she had to do.

Her eyes were dry as she looked at him, her face pale but composed. Tears were too shallow for emotions that rent the depths of her soul, and if she cried it would be in pity for herself, not empathy for him. No, tears were a waste of time.

So she simply looked at him, loving him, and she said calmly, "And the bottom line?"

There may have been a flicker of gratitude in his eyes; it may have been no more than acknowledgment of what he had expected from her. He said without flinching, "Statistically, five years at the outside. Probably much less. Not all of it will be easy. There will be hospitals and transfusions and chemotherapy, which makes me so sick I don't know or care where I am...and even then, there's no guarantee that I'll ever be as well as I am at this moment. There may never be another time when I can do what I am doing now, which is why this trip..." Here, for the first time, he almost stumbled, and he briefly avoided her eyes. "Meant so much to me," he continued softly. "There was so much I wanted to go and see, to make up for...to store against the time when memories are all I have. I didn't mean"—

and this was said so softly she had to strain to hear—"to involve you."

She stood, silently but steadily. The strength she found to do so surprised her. "But I am involved," she said quietly, firmly.

In the quick look he cast her was a mixture of panic and hope, and just as swiftly it was replaced with a steely rejection. "No," he said briefly. She could feel the tension building and see it tightening in his face and in his arms. "I don't want that. I won't do it to you—to us. I should have left without telling you, but"—anger threaded through his voice, impatience and frustration with himself—"how could I? I *love* you. . . . Damn it, it's not fair!" His breath was drawn in sharply through his teeth, and he whirled abruptly away from her, his hands clenching into fists and his shoulder muscles knotting across his back. "Not fair that I should meet you now—I tried so hard not to love you—now, when there's no time!"

Something stabbed through Jennifer then like a cold knife, something that seemed to slice her apart when she saw Adam for the first time in the grip of raw emotion. But she would not let it defeat her. If she gave in now, then neither of them had a chance. Her feet walked the few steps over to him; he flinched when she lightly touched his arm, and she let her hand drop. Then she touched him again, more firmly. "We can't change that," she said quietly. Was that her voice, so calm, so controlled? Was it she who was stating simple truths in such a clear, unembellished manner when all she wanted to do was lift her voice and scream to the heavens, decrying the unfairness of it all and begging someone to tell her it wasn't true? "We can't change time, and we can't change loving each other. We can only do the best we can with what we have."

He stared at her for a long time, as though she were a creature he had never seen before. She could not decipher the expression on his face—was it awe, repulsion, fear? Or hope? "Jenny..." His voice was hoarse. "You don't know what you're saying. Damn it, I'm *dying*! Every day, every minute, with every breath... I might have a year, or two, or I might have six months... six weeks! How can we make the best of what we have when we have nothing!"

And then, as she looked at the naked despair on his face, her own anger flared, and it caused tears to sting her eyes. "Do you think you're so different from the rest of us?" she flung back, tightening her grip on his arm and making him look at her. Her eyes glittered. "*None* of us knows how long we have—and maybe you're even a little luckier than most because you at least have an idea. Damn it, Adam, it doesn't make any difference; it doesn't make me love you less...." She drew a breath, gulping a little, lowering her eyes briefly to regain control.

Then she continued more calmly, "I've lived all my life with a disease for which there is no cure. Don't you think I know what it's like having something like that hanging over your head? No, what I have is not fatal by itself, but it could lead to an accident that could be fatal; it could get worse and leave me an invalid or a mental cripple the rest of my life. But it hasn't!" she insisted earnestly, her fingers pressing deeper into the taut flesh of his arm. "I've learned not to let it make a difference, and you will too, Adam. Don't let it take more from you than it already has."

The despair in his eyes turned slowly to wonder, then to helplessness ruled by yearning. "I can't—" he said brokenly, "ask you to love me...to watch me.... I wanted to take care of you," he said, and his hand trembled a little as he stroked her hair. His eyes were filled with such tenderness and sorrow that she could no longer hold back the tears. "Not the other way around...."

She pushed away, tears staining the pockets of her eyes and glittering in flakes of gold from the depths of eyes that were determined and unafraid. The small line of her mouth was tight, and her voice was steady as she said, "I don't need anyone to take care of me, Adam. I'm not offering you my pity, and I won't accept yours. All I want is to love you...."

Her voice almost broke on the last, and he turned away slowly. The quality of his sigh drifted across to her from a wide chasm of pain. "God," he said softly, wearily. "It was so easy before I met you. I mean, I thought I had finally learned to deal with it. I could let the anger go; I thought I had accepted the inevitable. A year, I thought. So I had a year, and I was going to use it doing everything, seeing everything, I would never be able to again. I thought it was a positive step; it was the best I could do. I wasn't fighting it anymore, I was just enjoying every minute to the fullest. And then you came along, and everything looked different. I saw my limits in you, because I wanted you forever, and I didn't have forever. I knew the memory of you would never be enough, and that brought the anger back. You made me see that all the while I had thought I had accepted my fate, what I was really doing was running, and time was my demon. It still is, Jenny." He turned. His face, lined with weariness, was sober, his eyes steady. "You haven't changed the facts; you've only made me see them more clearly. I don't like them, but I've accepted them. And all that leaves us is—"

"Loving each other," she said quietly.

"Yes," was all he said, and they looked at each other until at last, helplessly, the simplicity of their love drew them wordlessly into each other's arms. They held each other, quietly, solemnly, needing nothing but the moment while time crept by around them unnoticed.

"Oh, Jenny," he whispered at last, shakily. "Whenever I'm around you all I want is to hold you, and to love you. . . . You make me forget it's not forever. I just want to be with you and make it last as long as I can, and it's not fair to you."

She pushed away from him. "It *is* forever," she said fiercely. "I'll never stop loving you—you can't make me stop—and I won't let you stop loving me. . . ."

His arms tightened around her, and his lips

brushed across her forehead. "God, Jenny, how I do love you!" he whispered. She wound her arms around his neck tightly, so tightly that the muscles ached, and his return embrace crushed her chest and cut off her breath. When at last the embrace eased, he stepped away a little, still holding her, searching her face with anxiety and wonder in his eyes. "You've given me so much," he said softly. "How can I ask you for more? All I want is a few more weeks with you, to stay with you awhile longer, to be with you ... to pretend it never has to end...."

She looked up at him solemnly, her arms linked about his neck, and she said simply, "Love me, Adam."

They spent the afternoon tangled in each other's arms and legs, their lovemaking at first desperate and urgent and later so sweet it brought tears of sheer happiness to Jennifer's eyes. They sought each other again and again, unable to have enough, holding each moment of perfect union as a valiant fortress against the threat of time, growing stronger in the sharing, more certain with every discovery of the power of their love. At last exhaustion and a sleepless night took its toll on both of them, and Jennifer drifted away wrapped in the warmth of his arms and the blanket of his love.

When she awoke, she was alone.

The gasp that was torn from her came without volition; she sat upright in bed with fear pounding through her veins and a cry on her lips, and immediately Adam was beside her. "It's all right, love," he said soothingly, holding her. "I'm here. I'm sorry I frightened you."

"I—I thought you had left me!" she whispered, clinging to him.

He pushed her away gently, and his eyes were sober. "I told you I would never do that," he reminded her. "Not without saying good-bye."

She relaxed in his arms, her heart slowly resuming its normal rhythm, the confusion of her awakening draining away in the security of his presence. It was dark outside, but the lamp was on—Adam would not sleep without it—and she noticed that he was fully dressed. A new and vague alarm began to form within her at this, for if he wasn't leaving, why was he dressed? But as she was about to question, he suddenly pushed her away and commanded, "Get up; get dressed." His smile was secretive and excited. "And hurry—I want to show you something."

They stood outside in the darkness with the first snow of the year drifting down upon them in heavy, fluffy flakes, wrapped in the warm stillness of its silent spell, and Adam said softly, "Did you make this magic for me?"

She snuggled closer into the shelter of his arm about her shoulders, and the contentment of the world outside was only a reflection of what grew within her. It was magic. Everything was so still, she thought she could almost hear the flakes of snow drifting upon the water, and the darkness of the night was overcast with a surrealistic pearly glow. Only the two of them existed within this timeless cocoon of warmth and silence; it was as though the miracle of their love had been captured and reflected in the magic of this first snowfall.

He turned her to himself, his arms about her waist, and the quietness of his smile was illuminated in the gentle radiance of the snowfall, his eyes as clear as the purity of the night that surrounded them. The softness of his voice carried reverence for the moment. "I want to make love to you now more than anything else in the world," he said. "But"—his warm lips brushed across her cold nose—"I'm so hungry I don't think I have the strength. Would it be too much to ask...?"

She laughed and slipped her arm around his waist as they walked back inside. They made a cheese fondue before the fireplace and listened to the crackling of the logs and the cottony softness of the drifting snow outside, needing no words to enhance the completeness they shared. Later they did make love, slowly and wonderfully, adding one more perfect memory to their store against the future.

Chapter Nine

Jennifer awoke the next morning to warm kisses upon her eyelids, and a musical voice urging, "Wake up, sleepyhead; this is a working day."

She made a soft sound of pleasure and protest, drawing him to her without opening her eyes. She loved the feel of his morning nakedness against hers, the warmth of his lips upon her neck and his caressing hands on her waist. "Is it still snowing?" she murmured.

"Um-hmm. The tops of the trees look like they've been dusted with powdered sugar, and the ground looks like an empty canvas." He caught his breath and captured her exploring hands, saying firmly, if a little unsteadily, "None of that. You've got to go to work, and you've overslept."

She opened her eyes, smiling at him, and his own eyes lightened with pleasure and adoration as they moved over her sleep-flushed face, her tousled hair, her drowsy eyes. His smile was vague and wondering, as though it worked its way from his heart outward, and he said softly, "How is it possible that I can love you more every time I see you?"

Jennifer linked her arms around Adam's neck and drew his head down beside hers on the pillow, and that way they rested for a time, drinking in the fragrance and the presence of each other, wrapped in the still peace of the morning upon which nothing could intrude. And then he reluctantly moved away from her, sitting up, and kissed her forehead. "I mean it, love. I've got a hungry beast waiting for me next door, and though he was very polite to leave us alone last night, there is a limit to his tolerance." She opened her eyes, and she didn't seem to be able to stop smiling. An answering response lightened his eyes once again, and he ran one finger from the tip of her eyebrow along the outside path of her cheek, down to the corner of her mouth. "If you'll wait for me to shower," he suggested, "I'll drive you to work and we can even stop and have breakfast at the world-famous coffee shop in town."

"Sounds wonderful," she replied drowsily. "Shower here. I'll get dressed and feed the dog..." She turned over and pulled the blankets above her shoulders as he stood. "In a minute...."

He playfully slapped the blankets that covered the rounded curve of her bottom, but she only snuggled down deeper, awakening slowly and comfortably to the sound of the shower in the background and the memory of this warmth all around her. But she reluctantly admitted she had lingered too long, and just as she was throwing back the covers, a resounding knock echoed above the sound of running water to shatter the peace of the morning. At first she thought Bear had reached the end of his patience after all, but no, this was definitely a human knock. The only person she knew who would come out here at this hour of the morning was Jo, and she could not imagine what her sister wanted. She pulled on a terry-cloth robe and belted it as she pushed back her hair casually with her fingers and went to answer the door.

The sound of the shower ceased as she opened the door onto a cold, snow-frosted morning, and the silence seemed doubly acute as she stared at her callers. Joseph Underwood and Mrs. Patten stood against the fuzzy background veil of a fine shower of snow, their shoulders and their hair dusted with white, their faces surprised as they took in her appearance.

"I'm sorry, Jennifer," said Joseph awkwardly. "We didn't mean to wake you up; we thought... That is..." He deliberately looked over her shoulder as Jennifer made an embarrassed motion to draw the folds of her robe more securely over her chest. "We wanted to catch you before you went to the library. We thought it might be best if we talked to you at home."

"It will only take a moment, my dear," declared Mrs. Patten, and sailed through the door without waiting for an invitation. She was a large woman, florid-faced and silver haired, with a bosom shaped like the proverbial bow of a ship.

Her presence in any room commanded attention, and Jennifer could do nothing but lift her eyebrows in resignation and gesture that Joseph follow his overbearing companion inside.

"Would you like to have a seat?" invited Jennifer politely. "May I take your coats?"

"We won't be here that long," replied Mrs. Patten firmly. "I only came to hear for myself exactly what you intend to do"—with a flourish she presented a copy of *The Tale of Elias Cotton*—"with this piece of filth."

Jennifer tried to keep her temper, which was not easy to do after having been dragged from a warm bed by an uninvited and unwelcome caller at eight o'clock in the morning. "I don't know what filth you could be referring to, Mrs. Patten," she replied calmly. "All I see is a book."

The good lady's color rose appreciably, her eyes fired for battle. "So it's true!" she declared triumphantly. "You approve this trash, and you refuse to remove it from the shelves of our public library."

Jennifer took the book from her with a movement that was slow and deliberate. Her head was beginning to ache. This was not the way she had intented to start the morning. "As I told Reverend Underwood, I will not let one person's opinion dictate the reading habits of our entire community. As it happens, I do approve of a piece of literature that is well-written and meaningful, and I will not remove it, or anything like it, from the shelves."

"Well!" Mrs. Patten looked down upon her

from a superior height. "Young lady, I hope you realize what a serious thing you're doing. You are forcing us to take this over your head." It was a prospect she obviously relished. "There are many in this town who never approved of appointing one so young and so"—she savored the word—"*radical* to such an important position, and let me tell you now—"

"Jenny, did you—"

Adam came in from the bathroom, a towel wrapped around his waist and another draped across his shoulders; they all turned at the same moment, and he broke off. It was one of those scenes straight out of a situation comedy, and it would have been hilarious had it not been quite so unexpected and, from the expressions that crossed both Joseph's and Mrs. Patten's faces, so deadly serious.

Perhaps three heartbeats passed before Jennifer recovered herself. Then she said in a voice that was amazingly calm, "Mrs. Patten, I don't believe you've met Adam Wilson. Adam, Mrs. Patten and Reverend Underwood."

Mrs. Patten drew herself up to her full, victorious height, her face a gorgeous scarlet, her mouth grim, and her eyes alight with the greedy blaze of scandal. "Joseph," she said stiffly, "I think we had better go."

The shock and the disappointment that were in Joseph's eyes as he looked at her actually hurt Jennifer. He mumbled something of an apology, and Jennifer was sorry to have hurt him, but they were both gone before she could say anything.

"Jenny..." Adam's hands were upon her shoulders, his voice tight with contrition. "Love, I'm sorry. I had no idea...."

Jennifer turned, her fingers pressed to her lips to contain a giggle, her eyes dancing suddenly. "Did you see the expression on that old lady's face?" she exclaimed, and the giggle burst through.

His face relaxed, and a sparkle of amusement caught the corners of his own eyes. "It couldn't have been better if we had staged it," he admitted wryly. And then, more seriously, "I hope..."

She looped her arms about his neck and tilted her face up invitingly, unwilling to admit anything from the outside into the time they shared. "You promised me breakfast," she reminded him.

He lifted an eyebrow mockingly. "Do you really think it's wise that we be seen in public together after this?"

She shrugged. "There's no reason not to now. It will be all over town before noon." And she grinned impishly. "I always wanted to have a reputation to live up to."

He returned her grin and brushed his lips across her nose. "I'll do my best to oblige, ma'am."

"But Adam..." She looked at him in mock puzzlement, even though her eyes continued to sparkle. "Why in the world didn't you at least put on your pants?"

He returned her look soberly for a moment, and then, as one, they burst into helpless laughter. And as they held each other, laughing, the demons and the ghosts that lurked ever-present at the borders of their happiness vanished, for the moment, into the sparkle and glitter of a snowy morning. For just that moment they were free.

It wasn't until they left the coffee shop and walked across the street to the library that the clammy fingers of reality began to creep about Jennifer again. Why was it that whenever he was out of her sight, she became frightened? He had promised he would not leave without telling her; she had to trust him enough to believe that. But she knew the desperation that drove him, and whenever they were separated, she began to fear that their love was not enough to fight off his ghosts. How much longer could she go on, knowing that every day might be the day he left, knowing there was nothing she could do to stop him, no way she could reach him, for this was a battle he must fight for himself....

She tried to make her voice sound matter-of-fact as she said hesitantly, "What—will you do today?"

His smile read the anxiety that prompted the question and quietly reassured her of his promise. "I'm going to go home," he said, "and read, and play with my dog, and take pictures of the blackbird tracks in the snow." He brushed his lips across hers lightly. "I'll pick you up about five, okay?"

She nodded and restrained an urge to call out to him as she watched him go. How could they go on without talking about this? Nothing had been resolved between them yesterday, nothing. Now she knew the truth, but the truth had in no way freed them from its consequences. Still, he was caught in a desperate race against time, and she was just a stop along the way ... perhaps one he could not afford.

Over and over again she thought there must be something she could say, something she could do.... But what could she say to him? Could she change his fate, make him well? Could she promise him time? She spent the day scouring the medical textbooks and periodicals in the library, and she knew almost as much about the course of the disease as he did. Yes, there was a chance of permanent remission. At his age and in his circumstances the chances were good. But he was right to prepare himself for the worst; she would not cruelly beg him to cling to false hope. And neither would she deceive herself into believing they had nothing but a normal, long life ahead of them. He would never be strong; the treatments and the tests that lay ahead of him would be painful and debilitating, and even then there were no promises. No, the best she could do for him was to accept the truth and support him in his decision to do so ... and to make every moment they had together precious and unfettered by shadows of the future.

She knew there was nothing more she could do, nothing she could say, to help him through his crucible. There was his love, and there was his battle, and nowhere did the two intersect This was something he had to face for himself, and he did not want her with him if the worst came. He thought he was being kind. He did not understand that losing him now by his own choice would hurt her as much or more than losing him later to a power beyond the control of either of them. He did not understand that because she loved him, this had become her battle as well, and she must fight it in her own way, but fight it she would with or without his help. She could only pray that he would give her the time. . . .

It was late in the afternoon when the letter came. She read it incredulously, twice, before she began to comprehend its meaning. It was a summons for her to appear before the library committee to discuss the manner in which she executed her duties and her suitability for continuance as librarian. The meeting was scheduled for Friday, the day after Thanksgiving.

She couldn't believe it. She stared at the page, and her hands shook with anger and incredulity. She had held this position for four years, and no one had ever complained about her capabilities or discretion. And now because of one narrow-minded woman with tunnel vision. . . .

"It's a witch hunt!" she exclaimed to Adam not fifteen minutes later. "A plain old-fashioned witch hunt, and I will not submit to it."

"It doesn't seem to me you have much choice," replied Adam gravely. He had listened to her tirade throughout the short drive home, and with each word his face had grown more grim. She still was shaking with rage, and her color blazed as she got out of the car without waiting for his assistance and trudged through the thin layer of snow toward her house.

"How can they *do* this?" she seethed. Adam caught her arm as her foot slid on an unbroken crust of snow. "Do they think they can really do this? Book burning went out with Nazi Germany! I won't let them get away with this, Adam," she promised grimly, deftly inserting her key into the lock.

His eyes lit with admiration and amusement as he agreed mildly, "Damn right, you won't." She was having difficulty extracting the key from the lock, and he took it from her calmly, holding the door for her to precede him. "Something tells me your esteemed colleagues have no idea what they've gotten themselves into."

Bear had been waiting patiently on the front step for their return, now he politely shook the snow off his fur before following Adam inside. Jennifer paused to pet him absently. "I just can't believe it," she repeated quietly, and when she looked at Adam again, her eyes were troubled and hurt. "That the library committee would have taken her seriously, that they would threaten my job..."

He came over to her and placed his hands on her shoulders firmly. His eyes were quiet and strong. "You have nothing to worry about," he told her. "They can try to intimidate you, but you just remember you have something they don't."

She looked up at him uncertainly. The first outrage was gone, and fear was beginning to creep into its place. "What's that?"

He smiled at her gently. "Second sight," he

told her. "You can see the truth where other people only see the trappings, and your enemies are powerless against that."

She looked at him, and his quiet strength began to infuse itself into her body. He believed in her. And she was in the right. They couldn't get away with this. With courage, righteous indignation returned—more than indignation, churning fury at the stupidity, the utter blindness, of those she was up against—and she began to strip off her coat with shaking, clumsy fingers. "Yes," she said grimly, clenching her teeth against the blind rage that was assaulting her. Perhaps, on some subconscious level, she was aware that she was subjugating her anger and her fear for Adam into this new, so much more minor, problem. And it was good—for both of them. "I sometimes wonder if half the people in this town can even read, and they dare to judge me! They won't get away with this!"

In an angry motion she flung her coat away; the corner of it caught the base of a glass vase on the end table, and it tipped to the floor with a splintering crash. The sudden sound riveted Jennifer's attention; shiny fragments caught the reflection of sunbeams flooding through the window and magnified them into a glittering, erratic pattern. She pressed her fingers to her temples and tried to concentrate, tried to look away, but it was too late; she felt herself sinking, being drawn downward into herself, enveloped by the shimmery fog. . . .

". . . okay, Jenny?"

Adam's voice drifted down to her from a great distance; she felt his warm arms cradling her and his hand lightly against her hair. An overwhelming sense of defeat engulfed her; full of emptiness and shame, she staggered a little against him as she muttered, "Oh, no ... so stupid. ..."

"Hush." He bent and lifted her into his arms. "It's all right. Just hush now. Rest."

"Don't," she protested as he carried her toward the bedroom. "Your arm ..."

"My arm is fine." His voice was reassuring, strong. He laid her down upon the bed, and she knew nothing else until she awoke and he was sitting beside her, gently coaxing her back to him with his smile.

She turned her head, tears of shame and defeat pricking her eyes. She had wanted to be so strong for him; she had wanted to convince him that she was able and willing to handle whatever life had to offer. ... He did not need her problems as well as his. What did she expect of him, anyway? Didn't he have enough to deal with on his own without having an invalid lover on his hands? He had been right all along; there was nothing for them, no future, she could not ask him to take on her weakness when his life was already so complicated by personal tragedy. ...

He took her chin between his thumb and forefinger and turned her face firmly toward him. She could not blink back the tears quickly enough, and there was surprise and confusion in his eyes. "Say, what is this?" he demanded softly. "Didn't we go through this all before? There's no reason for you to be ashamed around me, or to hide from me.... Don't you know that?"

She swallowed thickly and blinked back the tears, struggling to sit up. "I-I'm sorry," she managed. "I didn't want you to—"

"Did you do it on purpose?" he challenged gently. "Is it something you can control?"

She shook her head mutely, and his hand stroked her cheek tenderly. "Then stop apologizing. Stop trying to shut me out of a part of your life. I share your problems and your hurts as well as all the good things about you. I can't help it, because I love you."

He must have realized at the same moment as she what his words meant, because a film of distance closed over his eyes when he saw the pleading in hers. Why couldn't he realize that she shared his problems too, that they were as much an inextricable part of her as her own were, and he could not shut her out? He wanted to help her, to stand by her and support her in the bad times as well as the good, but he would not allow her to do the same for him. With all her might she tried to make him see that, to know it in the urgency of her eyes and by the touch of her hand on his arm, and she said softly, "I love you too, Adam."

Slowly his eyes closed against the pain that had gathered there, rejecting the depth of her meaning even as he bent to brush her lips with a kiss, and he whispered, "I know."

"Adam..." Her fingers tightened on his arm, and desperation was in her tone. She must try to reach him, to make him see....

"No." The finger he pressed to her lips was firm, and so was his tone. In his eyes and in his face was the firmly established distance again, although his voice was softened with a plea for patience. "No looking into the future today," he said. "There's too much"—he dropped his eyes—"too much I don't want to see," he admitted. "Too much confusion. Jenny..." He looked at her, and through the pain and sorrow in his eyes was a plea for her understanding. "I have to deal with this on my own. If you love me, give me the time to do that. Please."

She looked at him, and though her heart was breaking, she could say nothing. If that was all he asked of her, then that was all she could give him. Time.

Jo Ellen was in the library first thing the next morning. "I can't talk about it now, Jo," Jennifer said firmly. "Not here."

Jo Ellen took her arm and without another word escorted her into the back room. Her face was grim with concern and her voice low. "I couldn't believe it," she said despairingly. "Jennifer, what have you done?"

"What have *I*...?" After a moment of incredulity Jennifer shook her head and sank in resignation to a dusty, hardback chair. She should have known. Poor little Jennifer, incompetent, in need of shelter, unable to function on her own.... Jo Ellen loved her but had absolutely no faith in her, for to Jo Ellen Jennifer was just her helpless little sister in constant need of protection and guidance.

"Now, Jenny," Jo Ellen said with a breath, loosening her muffler and dusting snow off her sleeves, "I know with a little effort and a lot of tact we can clear this misunderstanding up. I've already talked to the members of the committee, and they are all willing to—"

"You did what?" Jennifer sprang from her chair, her eyes wide with disbelief and her color high. Jo Ellen took a startled step backward. "You had no right to do that, Jo!" she cried. "This is my fight, and I'll see it through my way, on my own! For goodness sake, can't you see that I'm grown up now, and there are some things I have to do on my own?"

Jo looked cautiously hurt, very confused. "Jenny, I don't think you understand the seriousness..."

Jennifer took a calming breath, sorry she had shouted at her sister. "I understand," she said briefly, meeting her eyes evenly. "I understand my job is at stake, but it's a lot more than that; so are basic rights and freedoms, and those are what I have to fight for." She sighed, her expression softening. "I know you only want to help, Jo. I know you only mean the best for me. But I've made my stand, and I won't back down."

Jo Ellen looked at her for a moment, and Jennifer could read the emotion warring on her face. Apparently she decided, however, that Jennifer was in no mood at present to be persuaded or bullied, guided or reasoned with. She knew Jennifer's temperament and had had experience dealing with all of her moods, but she had never seen her sister quite so determined about anything before. Her expression gentled, and she said soothingly, "Perhaps this isn't quite the best time to talk about it. You must still be upset; this has all been a shock for you. You need some time to calm down, to think about it; I'm sure you'll see reason. And when you do..."

Jennifer shook her head, once again firmly.

Jo Ellen looked puzzled and impatient for just a moment; then she quickly wiped that expression from her face too. "Will we see you and Adam at dinner tomorrow?" she inquired pleasantly.

Jennifer could not help notice that there was a barbed edge to that apparently innocent inquiry. She replied cautiously, "If we're still invited."

Jo Ellen released a long-suffering sigh. "Of course you're still invited. I wouldn't take back an invitation just because—"

She broke off, and Jennifer inquired mildly, "Just because what?"

Jo Ellen looked disturbed, apologetic. "Jenny," she said carefully, "you know how people in this town talk. You should know"—she looked uncomfortable—"that there are some nasty rumors going around about you two."

Jennifer almost smiled. "They sure didn't waste any time, did they?" she murmured.

Jo Ellen hesitated. "So?" she prompted.

On this subject Jennifer wanted to confide in her sister. She wanted to tell her everything, she wanted Jo Ellen, who was always so wise and competent, to tell her everything was going to be all right. She wanted Jo Ellen to look at all the facts and somehow find a solution. Because this, the most important thing in her life, she could not handle alone, she didn't want to handle alone. She desperately needed help and strength . . . but she knew that this was the one thing no one could help her with.

She said simply, very softly, "I can't, Jo."

Jo Ellen must have read the entire story in Jennifer's face before she turned away. The silence reminded Jennifer that she had few secrets from her sister, and when she at last ventured a glance at her, Jo Ellen's face was softened with thoughtfulness and concern. She said quietly, "You're in love with him, aren't you?"

Jennifer could only nod, and the truth of it was in her eyes.

For another moment Jo Ellen was silent. "It doesn't seem to be making you very happy."

Jennifer wanted so badly to cry out her troubles on her sister's shoulder that she had to clench her fists to keep from doing so. She swallowed back a sudden lump in her throat and said carefully, "There are . . . complications."

She could not escape her sister's penetrating gaze. "Would those complications have anything to do with the way he feels about you?"

"No, Jo, it's nothing like that; it's just . . ." Jennifer's face was torn with pain and the need to confide. But she couldn't. This was her problem, hers and Adam's; she could not rely upon anyone else to solve it for her. "Please, Jo," she entreated.

Jo Ellen was torn between the desire to help and

the demand Jennifer made for privacy. "Honey, you've only known him for a month," she said gently. "I just don't want to see you hurt."

"Being hurt is part of being alive," Jennifer answered. And then she managed a reassuring smile. "I know what I'm doing," she said. "Really. Don't worry, okay? We'll see you tomorrow."

Everyone who came into the library that day knew about the "scandal," and Jennifer endured the entire range of sentiments in reaction. People who had not been inside the library since they graduated high school came in just to see the kind of pornography with which she was stocking the shelves. Others wanted only to gossip, to offer pretend sympathy and to inquire what her plans were after she left the library. In their eyes was a sort of cautious skepticism, as though they had never really seen her before and could hardly believe what they were seeing now. Still others—and these were the worst—came to inform Jennifer that they had never approved of the type of material their children had been reading and held her solely responsible, and that they considered the action being taken now long overdue. This both hurt and frightened Jennifer. She was not used to being the victim of public criticism. She had been loved and protected and sheltered all her life, and she was not used to fighting. No one ever said a harsh word to Jennifer; no one had ever demeaned or threatened or criticized her, and she did not know how to deal with any of it now. Yet she was to go before a committee and defend her principles before people who had declared themselves her enemies. . . . For the first time the reality of it sank in, and Jennifer actually had to leave the desk and sit down, unable to face one more curious or unfriendly face, shocked and appalled by her own vulnerability.

All her life she had wanted no more than to stand on her own, to make her own decisions and to be accountable for her own life. But with such privileges came responsibilities, and this was the first time Jennifer had ever been called upon to pay her dues. It was her test by fire; she must endure it alone . . . and she was very frightened.

But she tried to keep all of this from showing on her face when she met Adam that afternoon. The thought of being with him again was all that had sustained her throughout the day, and she did not want to admit intrusive unpleasantness into the precious time they shared together. She sometimes felt as though she were living three lives: One as a sort of small-town Joan of Arc risking her job and her livelihood for her principles; another as a silent partner in suffering with the man she loved, fearing every moment of losing him; and the other, quite simply, as a woman in love with all the joy, pain, and uncertainty common to that condition. She tried very hard to keep those lives separate, not seeing that they were, in fact, all part of the same.

Adam was wearing dark sunglasses that afternoon, and they made his face look even paler. She tried not to scrutinize him, tried not to feel that lurch of alarm as she wondered whether he was feeling worse, but he saw it in her eyes, and he smiled a little. "My eyes are sun-sensitive after all that medication, and the glare of the snow gives me a headache," he explained gently, touching the glasses. "Just another one of life's little inconveniences." Though she could not see his eyes, she could feel him watching her, examining her reaction, and she felt as though she had failed a test. It was not easy to be what he expected of her. It would never be easy.

She did not know what to say. Did he expect her to pretend it didn't matter, that she did not care? She did care. How could she not suffer with him when she knew the pain that every day of his limited time cost him; how could he expect her to keep her pain from him? She was afraid that anything she might say would be misinterpreted as sympathy, so in the end she said nothing.

"I did have some good news today though," he said more cheerfully as he started the car. "I sent the last of the photographs to Jake, and he telegraphed his approval—in fact, his enthusiasm—just this afternoon." He glanced at her. "That was your cue to say 'Congratulations.'"

Something within Jennifer tightened in apprehension. She said, careful to keep her tone noncommittal, "Does that mean ... your work here is finished?"

"I guess it does." But his reply was absentminded, as though he were thinking of something else, and he suddenly gave a small, rather wondering laugh. "You know, I was just thinking ... about how that book will be around long after ..." Jennifer knew he did not finish that sentence for her sake, not his own. "About," he amended, "how people will be reading it for generations to come, whether or not I'm around to see. It's a strange feeling. I hope it's as good as Jake says it's going to be."

The pall began to fall over them as the misty veil upon the future was lifted a fraction to reveal the bleak and unrelenting landscape that lay ahead. Once again Jennifer felt helpless, frustrated, torn with yearning to help and to reassure, but completely impotent. He had asked her for time. He wanted no pressure. She had no right to demand anything from him—not even that he allow her to brighten his future with the promise of her love. Then what *could* she do to help?

He glanced at her, and the expression of emptiness and distance that had come over his face was suddenly replaced with gentle concern that locked him into the present. "Did you have a bad day?" he inquired.

Was that it, then? Was that what she could do for him—just give him the space to show his love and his concern for her, to allow him to share in her life for as long as possible? But why, then, *why* couldn't he see that she needed the same thing from him? All she asked from him was the chance to share her love . . . and all he asked from her was the chance to share his.

She smiled a little weakly and replied, "Not one I'd choose to live over. I'm . . . not used to being disapproved of."

He looked at her soberly as he pulled in front of

her house and put the car into gear. "It's not going to be easy for you, is it?"

She hesitated. She did not want to burden him with her problems. She did not want him to see her weaknesses. She wanted to be brave and strong and perfect for him.... She dropped her eyes, smiling a little. "No," she admitted softly. "I guess—it's going to be the hardest thing I've ever done."

His gloved hand closed over hers, and with a gentle pressure he drew her to him until their foreheads were touching. He had removed the glasses when he parked the car, and his eyes were very clear. There was a teasing confidence in his smile. "You know something?" he said. "I'm not worried. The only people who have a right to be worried are the ones on that committee. They don't know," he added softly, tracing an outline with his gloved fingertip from the center of her forehead to the tip of her nose, "that this is one woman who always gets what she wants, and we mere mortals are helpless under her power."

Jennifer wrapped her arms about him and offered him her lips and tried not to let him know how very, very mortal she felt. For he held within his power the one thing she wanted, the only thing of importance to her, and she was helpless against the feeling that time was running out....

Chapter Ten

Thanksgiving was a strained, rather gloomy meal, as everyone's attention was more on the ordeal facing Jennifer than on the festivities at hand. Jennifer did everything she could to lighten the atmosphere of impending doom, for she had wanted so badly for this day with Adam to be special and unspoiled. She tried not to think that it might well be the last holiday they shared. She wanted to relax with him and her family and see it as only one in a long line of holidays and family get-togethers. . . . She wanted, for just one more day, to close her eyes and imagine everything was as perfect as their love should make it. Adam, instinctively sharing her sentiment, was her ally, and for a time it worked. At first Phillip's protective instincts bristled at Adam's presence, and even Jo, apparently influenced by rumors of evil behavior on their part, was a little bit more reserved than Jennifer had expected. But the couple's contentment with each other was expansive, and Adam, when he chose to be charming, was irresistible. Soon their host and hostess began to thaw, and for a time the holiday seemed almost normal.

But over coffee before the fireplace Phillip could not contain himself any longer. His face fell into the lines of a worried scowl that even the memory of his wife's elaborate meal could not ease, and he demanded without preamble, "Jennifer, for God's sake, what are you thinking of?"

"Turkey," replied Jennifer with a mischievous grin. "I think I'll probably be thinking about turkey from now until Christmas."

Phillip released an impatient breath. "Do you, by any remote stretch of the imagination, realize that your job is at stake here? Your whole career? What will you do if you lose your job?"

Jennifer wondered if the real reason Phillip was so concerned was his fear that if his sister-in-law became unemployed, she would be dependent on him. But it was an unworthy thought, unfair to Phillip, who had been so good to her, and she was ashamed of herself. She tried to subdue her impatience with him, and she told him calmly, "I hope it won't come to that, Phil. It would be a great miscarriage of justice if it did, and I've got to believe that the people who appointed me are more fair-minded than that."

"But why take the chance?" he insisted, distressed. "Over one trashy book! Jennifer, I think you've lost your mind!"

Jennifer lifted an eyebrow, and she felt Adam move restlessly in his seat next to her on the sofa. "You've read it?" she inquired of her brother-in-law.

"Everyone in town has read it by now," he replied impatiently, and Jennifer could not help smiling.

"So what's the point," she inquired reasonably, "of taking it off the shelves? I always said there was nothing like a good scandal to make a book into a best seller."

Phillip scowled, and Jo Ellen interrupted. "Jennifer, you know very well what we mean. Why set yourself up for this... pain, and humiliation, over something so trivial? You don't need the stress. It's so unimportant, and there's too much at stake."

Jennifer had to count to ten. A glance at Adam's face showed his lips compressed, and his eyes very active. He wanted to help her, he wanted to speak up for her, but he sensed it was her fight, and he gave her the freedom to conduct it on her own. She loved him for that.

Jennifer took a breath. "I happen to consider irresponsible censorship a very important issue," she said, her eyes darkening. "I also consider it part of my job to defend against just that when it threatens our community. I—"

"Irresponsible!" Phillip exclaimed heatedly. "Now you've hit the nail on the head! You don't think it's irresponsible of you to make a federal case out of one R-rated book?"

Jennifer tried to keep the angry pace of her breathing under control. Her eyes met Adam's, and she found strength in his silent encouragement. "If a federal case is what it takes," she assured him calmly, "yes."

Phillip made a sound of repressed exasperation

and anger, and even Jo Ellen seemed to retreat a reluctant, despairing distance from her. When Phillip looked at her his eyes were cold. "You're wrong about this, Jenny," he said. "Dead wrong."

"Oh, Jenny," Jo Ellen put in sadly. "You know we love you, but we just can't back you on this. I'm sure if you would just take the time to think about it, you'd see that we're right, and it's just not worth it...."

Jenny felt a slow, cold emptiness fill her, and the only thing that kept the tears from flooding her throat was the steady look in Adam's eyes. She simply shook her head, and the subject was closed.

"Well," she said weakly to Adam when they arrived home, "even my own family's against me."

He stroked her shoulder reassuringly. "They're doing what they think is right, just as you are."

She managed to smile at him. "Thanks, for not jumping to my defense. I could tell you wanted to, but..."

His fingers threaded gently through the hair at her temples. Jennifer thought she could live on the light in his eyes alone for the rest of her life. "There are some battles," he told her, "that a person just has to fight alone."

The meaning behind his words was painfully clear, and she stepped wordlessly into his arms. Yes, she thought. This was hers, and he had his. And the best they could do for one another was to let each meet his or her dragon on his own terms, for victory any other way would be meaningless.

"Oh, Adam," she whispered. "Why does it

have to be so complicated?'' It would be so easy for her to just back away from this fight, or to let someone else carry her standard for her. Between Phillip and Jo, they could have persuaded the library committee to ignore Mrs. Patten. All Jennifer had to do was recall one book, and the entire terrifying mess would be forgotten. But she couldn't back down from her position, and she couldn't accept help from anyone else . . . any more than Adam could accept her help as he went through his own ordeal.

''I know how hard this is for you,'' Adam said, and she believed that he really did. ''I know how much courage it's going to take to do what you have to do.'' He brushed her hair with a kiss. ''No matter what happens, I want you to know that I'm already proud of you, and that I'll never forget the brave woman who went up against a lynch mob armed with nothing more than the truth and a fetching smile.'' There was gentle teasing in his eyes, but a serious meaning behind his words, and Jennifer did not feel brave at all. *He would never forget her.* Was that enough? How could it be?

She pressed her face into his shoulder, holding him as if with that physical motion she could keep him from slipping away from her. ''Oh, Adam,'' she whispered shakily. ''I'm scared to death.''

His arms tightened about her; his lips were warm and firm in the kiss he placed against her face. ''Just remember,'' he assured her, ''you won't be going through this alone.''

She pressed herself to him, desperately grateful

for that but yearning for more... to have him in her life forever, by her side with his silent, watchful support, ready to steady her when she stumbled and to hold her hand when she passed through fire. And more, she wanted to do the same for him....

The morning was snow-blindingly bright and designed to instill courage as Adam drove her silently to the library. The committee met in the dark and dusty wood-paneled conference room, twelve members gathered around a scuffed table—like a jury, Jennifer thought somewhat distractedly. Mrs. Patten held a prominent position at the head of the table, Joseph Underwood at her side, victoriously ready to present her case. Adam took a chair at the back of the room with Jo Ellen and Phillip and a few other interested observers. Jennifer caught the smile of encouragement in her sister's eyes that lit a spark in her heart as she took her own seat.

Jennifer maintained every appearance of outward composure as she listened to the charges brought against her. She thought she would be all right if only her heart would stop pounding. And how could she say anything in her own defense when her throat was so dry she could hardly swallow? She looked at the faces of long-time friends, acquaintances and coworkers and an awful, empty despair crept over her as one by one they refused to meet her eyes. It was a witch hunt. They had tried and found her guilty long before this meeting, and she did not have a chance....

Like a well-rehearsed drama, the proceedings went on without her. She knew that a judgment would be made first upon the books in question, and then the issue of her suitability for continued employment would arise—and that the result of the second was linked inextricably to the outcome of the first. Pillar by pillar her defense fell as one book after the other was found unsuitable for display upon the shelves of the public library. *Elias Cotton* was the first to go, of course, with no debate or question. Jennifer's despair mounted as, in rapid succession, there followed the works of Thomas Wolfe, Lord Byron.... Then the past year's best-seller list was stripped methodically and without question, one book after another, in swift, mechanical execution. Jennifer felt like a mesmerized spectator before the guillotine, helpless, unheard, sickened into numbness with each new fall of the blade.

At last Winston Andrews, president of the school board and senior member of the committee, removed his glasses and looked at Jennifer gravely. "I find this most appalling, Miss Kiel," he said. "It has been our custom to trust the judgment of our librarian when it came to spending the city's money and stocking our shelves, but I'm forced to admit that...recent revelations make it necessary for us to reexamine our position...and in the process, to reexamine your position in relationship to that trust."

This was her moment, her one and only chance to say something in her own defense. She prayed that her voice would not break into the fine quivering that was working its way through every muscle of her body, and that it could be heard over the pounding of her heart. She managed, "Mr. Andrews, if I might say something..."

"I hardly think," interrupted Mrs. Patten in a clear, decisively vicious tone, "that anything you have to say could possibly be of interest to this committee. Your actions have spoken quite well for themselves." And she turned to face the members of the committee, upon whose good will and good faith Jennifer had been relying. The woman's eyes reminded Jennifer of a wolf's who had cornered a rabbit and was savoring the victory before moving in for the kill. "After all," she declared triumphantly, "how much debate can there be about the suitability of this woman for a position that places her in control of the moral fiber of this community when she is at this moment living in sin with a man who makes his living taking pornographic photographs of naked women?"

There was a moment of shocked silence in which Mrs. Patten looked down upon the assembly in righteous superiority and benevolent confidence. It took a moment for even Jennifer to comprehend what she had said, and then she felt her color drain, to be replaced in a moment by a swift sting of heat that scorched a path from one cheek to the other and left the rest of her cold and shaking. There was a murmur of horror and distaste mixed with agreement, much shuffling of feet, and heads turning. Jennifer felt as though she had been stripped naked and placed upon a platform before the entire town, and the censure and disapproval of her friends and relatives were the stones they hurled. She saw Adam, his face dark and his fists clenched; she saw him start to leap to his feet.

And then Joseph Underwood's voice cut across the nightmare, calm and authoritative, focusing all attention upon himself. "Miss Kiel is not on trial here," he said, "for either real or imagined crimes, and her personal life has no place in this discussion. I sugget that we confine ourselves to the subject at hand."

Jennifer looked at him, and with the gratitude that flooded her came a new strength, a strange calm. What had it cost him to defend her when he above all people had been hurt by her? She knew he did not approve of her relationship with Adam, and he had been shocked and offended when he had discovered them together. He had made it clear that he disagreed with her position on *Elias Cotton,* yet he now defended her right to express her opinion. Which was, in fact, the basis of this entire issue—personal freedom.

The disapproval and distaste were now directed at Mrs. Patten, as the other members of the committee agreed with the minister and were happy not to be forced to delve into such a sticky subject. The woman retired somewhat huffily, greatly disgruntled, to the backstage of the action momentarily, and when Jennifer met Adam's eyes, calm, supportive and confident, the last of her fears and her uncertainties vanished.

She said, with a very gracious smile at Mrs. Patten, "I was only wondering if—while I'm still a member of this committee—I might offer a few words that might shed some light on this situation."

Mr. Andrews, anxious to be fair and obviously uncomfortable with the entire chain of events, urged, "Yes. Yes, of course."

Jennifer smiled at him. Suddenly she felt very calm inside. She linked her hands before her on the table and said, "I just want to make sure you all understand the librarian's problem. We have a very limited amount of shelf space, and it is the librarian's function to fill that space with a discriminating choice of material. I make decisions every day about how we can receive the most literary and educational value for our dollar, and if I've made mistakes"—she lifted her shoulders prettily and gracefully—"I am sorry. But you must see that it is not entirely my fault that this happened." At the looks of confusion and murmurs of protest, she held up one finger in a calming gesture. "You see," she explained, "the problem with this library system is that we have no written guidelines for the librarian to follow. It's a small system, and I suppose we always felt that there was no need for written rules, that the librarian's judgment was sufficent. However"—her smile was self-deprecating—"obviously it is not enough. I assure you that I would have been quite willing to abide by such regulations had they ever been presented to me in an official manner, so allow me to suggest, for my sake—or that of my successor—that we erase the ambiguity right now and vote on a standard of criteria by which books should be judged so that this unfortunate situation never recurs."

That seemed like a reasonable suggestion. Relief went around the table that Jennifer, far from causing an embarrassing scene, was approaching this entire matter in a very professional manner. Feelings softened toward her, and her proposal was embraced with enthusiasm. Jennifer glanced toward Adam, and his eyes were twinkling in quick, unmistakable perception. She felt a thrill of heady victory buoy her, that out of all the people in the room, he and only he had the insight to understand what she was doing, that he was applauding her silently, that he was behind her one hundred percent. Whatever happened, it was worth it all for that one moment of shared understanding and victory.

Jennifer took out a note pad on which she had been doodling aimlessly throughout the entire incredible ordeal. She said, "I've been making some notes on the standards by which you've reviewed and rejected the previous books, and if there are no objections, I would like to present these as formal criteria which, as they are voted upon, will stand permanently as a standard by which all library books are judged." Again there was a murmur of consultation and rapid agreement, and Jennifer was given permission to proceed. "First," she said, "I believe you made reference to 'offensive language and sexual themes.' Shall we agree that this should be number one on the list of unacceptable material to appear in a library book?"

There was unified agreement.

Jennifer made a check on her note pad and reached to take a book from the stack she had collected and placed upon the chair next to her. "*The Complete Works of William Shakespeare,* ladies and gentlemen," she said, and tossed it onto the pile of previously rejected books. "I can't imagine how you missed it. Don't worry, though," she assured them above one or two shocked looks and the stifled beginning of a murmured protest, "it's not your job to be familiar with everything on the shelves. I'll help you out as we go along."

Then, matter-of-factly, before anyone could say anything, she went on, "Graphic violence, evil intent, works reflecting the influence of drugs or alcohol or advocating their usage?"

Now there was a cautious silence. Some of the members present were becoming suspicious, and Jennifer prompted, meeting them eye for eye, "Yes or no?"

Obviously she had trapped them. They had agreed to set down criteria, and these were the criteria they had previously used. Murmured consultation agreed that this was a fair standard, one from which they refused to back away, and the decision came firmly, "Yes."

"Accepted then." Jennifer made another check on her pad, and reached for another book. *"The Collected Works of Edgar Allan Poe,"* she said, tossing the book into the stack. "As a matter of fact, I hope someone on this committee will take it upon himself to speak with the school board"—she smiled meaningfully at Mr. Andrews—"regarding the fact that Mr. Poe's works are still being taught in the classroom. It's a well-known fact that the man was a hardened drug addict and a psychotic, and the evil themes that are portrayed so graphically in his works can hardly be a good influence on our children.''

Jennifer could not help reflecting with vague amazement over the fact that men so indiscriminately condemning of Wolfe and Salinger would nonetheless hold a soft spot in their hearts for "The Raven" and "The Pit and the Pendulum." Mr. Andrews scowled and removed his glasses, prepared to do battle. "Young lady, you are manipulating this committee—"

"I am only giving you a chance to formally approve the criteria by which you have already banned books," Jennifer replied evenly. "I thought we had agreed this was the only way in which to effectively manage the future purchase of books on behalf of the township."

Again the murmur of confusion and uncomfortable agreement went around the room. "We must have guidelines," Jennifer reminded them.

No one could answer her.

She said, "Then, shall we agree that in the future no book containing explicit sex, offensive language, references to improper relationships or perversion, graphic displays of violence, or themes that condone immoral behavior be admitted to the shelves, and that all such books as now occupy space on the shelves of our public library be immediately removed?''

For just a moment there was silence. Suspicion and uneasiness permeated the atmosphere of the room, but what could they say? At last someone ventured, "Seems pretty cut and dried to me."

Another agreed. "Sounds fair."

And another, "It's what we wanted in the first place."

And Mrs. Patten's voice resounded, "Agreed."

A relieved murmur of consensus followed her lead.

Jennifer stood slowly and placed a copy of the Bible on top of the stack of banned books. Then she turned, and only ringing silence followed her as she walked out of the room.

Adam caught her on the snow-covered sidewalk, his laughter ringing in her ears and the sky spinning in a brilliant array of blue and black-striped branches as he lifted her off her feet and whirled her around. "Congratulations," he cried, "on your reinstatement!"

"That soon?" she gasped, struggling to regain her footing, and her startled laughter died as the import of his statement registered. "Adam, did they really ... ?"

His eyes were snapping with excitement and pride as he held her shoulders. "The door hadn't even closed behind you before all hell broke loose inside that room. Jenny, you were brilliant. I was so proud of you."

Jennifer could barely control all the emotions that were flaring and racing and bursting inside her—the shaky, incredulous relief, the intoxication of victory, the glowing confidence, the wondrous joy—but above it all was the look in Adam's eyes. *He was proud of her.* He had been there, supporting her, cheering for her, and she had not let him down. She wanted to hold on to that look for the rest of her life, to know that he was there for her always, as she would be for him, winning victories and slaying the foes that threatened their happiness. She had never loved him more. She did not think it was possible to be happier.

The doors of the library opened, and Jennifer saw Phillip and Jo heading the crowd that turned toward them. "Oh, quick," she said, slipping her arm around Adam's waist. "Let's go home." Her smile was radiant as she looked up at him; her arm tightened joyfully around his waist. "I don't want to share this moment with anyone but you."

Jenny was still laughing when they got out of the car, drunk on power, expansive with joy, embracing the moment wholeheartedly. "I still can't believe it worked! I think we should call the *Sixty Minutes* crew first thing in the morning. 'Small-Town Librarian Wins Battle Against Censorship'—I can see it now!"

Bear came bounding across the snow to meet them, responsive to Jennifer's bubbling mood, and Jennifer played tag with him all the way to the back door. Once inside the kitchen she knelt and hugged him fiercely, burying her face in his cold fur and laughingly delineating her victory to him step by step. Then she looked up at his master, her color high and her eyes dancing joyfully, and declared, "For goodness sake, take your coat off—we have to celebrate!" She leaped to her feet. "How about some hot spiced cider—sorry

about the shortage of Champagne. No!" She
whirled suddenly, placing her hands on his shoulders, her own high mood completely obscuring
what might have been a lack of response in him.
"Keep your coat on—I know what I want to do! I
want to go hiking through the woods and cut
down a Christmas tree! We can bring it back and
decorate it this afternoon, just the two of us, and
I'll make popcorn...."

"Jenny."

She had been so excited, so happy and full of
her own contentment, that she had not noticed
his lengthening silences on the way home, nor the
vagueness that had come over him, signaling his
thoughts were no longer with the events of the
morning—that perhaps they were no longer with
her at all. But now it was impossible to ignore the
strain on his face, the pain in his eyes, and it
struck her like a dousing with ice water as he
gently removed her hands from his shoulders and
pressed them together between his palms. "Jenny, please," he said quietly.

She felt everything within her draining slowly
away into numbness; she could read the expression on his face, but she could not accept what it
meant. The crystal day that spilled through the
window suddenly dulled; the buoyant celebratory
mood that once pervaded twisted and turned and
took on the trappings of a nightmare; and her
heart began to beat one incessant rhythm: *No ...
no ... no ...*

"Jenny," he began painfully, his hands tightening upon hers, "these last few days with you,

watching your courage against all the odds, being with you and sharing with you, have meant more to me than anything in my life." His eyes lightened and darkened with reluctance and admiration as they went anxiously over her face. "And it was as though, being with you, and sharing in it, gave me my own sort of courage—to face what I have to face, in my own way, unafraid. I never would have let you go through this alone," he assured her, "but now..." He dropped his eyes and reached into his pocket. He placed something small and metallic in her hand, and his smile was very weak. "My lease is up. This is good-bye, Jenny."

She stood staring at the key in her hand for a long time, trying to adjust, trying to believe it, trying not to fall apart. This was it. This was really it. She had known all along it must happen, but she had never imagined it really would.... He was leaving her. He was really leaving her, and there was nothing she could do to stop him. Where had her courage gone?

"Jenny, I..." Adam's voice was low and strained. She could not look at him. "You've given me so much. I stayed here because I was looking for a miracle, and I found...so much more than I ever expected. You've...given me a different kind of sight, the kind that makes the future look less frightening, and...everything will be brighter for me now because I've known you. I..."

She could take it no longer. What was the use in being strong when he was leaving her? Why should she hide from him and try to protect him from her feelings? It didn't matter anymore, not any of it.... She looked up at him, the key clenched in her hand, her eyes glittering. "You said you loved me," she accused.

His face was torn with pain and frustration, and his eyes pleaded with her for something—understanding, support, permission to leave—she didn't know. And then she didn't care, because she could not give him any of those things. "Jenny, please understand, it's because I love you that I have to do this! You've got to know that. I explained it all to you before—I can't ask you to live with this, I couldn't do that to your life."

"Oh, how very noble of you!" she cried. Her hand clenched around the key until her nails cut into her palm, though she hardly felt it. Her voice was high and shaking, and the hot tears blurred her vision and thickened her voice, but she could not control them; she did not even try. "You're always so quick with the self-sacrifice, aren't you? Well, let me tell you something, Adam Wilson, you're not so noble as you think you are! You're selfish, thoughtless, and self-centered; you'll take whatever you can, but you won't give anything in return! You say you love me, but you won't share yourself with me; you won't let me love you; you wrap yourself in a protective shield and you take away from me the only thing that *I* need, that I want. You don't love me! You don't even know what the word means! Six months, a year, fifty years—it doesn't matter, it's all the same! Because love means sharing, giving, every part of yourself.

"Love means sharing the good times as well as the bad. It's what you wanted from me, and I've given it to you, but you won't let me share in your problems. You won't let me into that part of your life. Oh, no, that's your exclusive territory, and no one is allowed to suffer over it but you!" She caught a trembling breath and made no effort to wipe away the tears that now streamed down her face unchecked. "Well, I suffered," she told him. "I suffered for you and with you, but mostly because of you, because you wouldn't let me love you. I can't give you back your health, Adam," she said, and once again her breath caught with a choked sound in her throat. But her eyes were steady, tear-blurred, and defiant. "I can't promise you *forever* any more than you can promise it to me. All I can give you is the best that I have for whatever time we have left. But that's not enough for you, is it?"

He took a breath, raw pain twisting his face as he took a hesitant step toward her. He made a half-formed movement as though to touch her, but his arm fell slowly back to his side. In his eyes was a desperate plea, reluctance and need, confusion and hurt, and something else—an anxiousness that leaped out to her and asked her for... what? Jennifer was too blinded by pain and anger and sorrow to see. "Jenny, I..." His voice was hoarse. "I never realized...."

She pressed her fingers to her face, stiffly rubbing away tears, desperately fighting for control, and each breath was a silent shudder. The confusion and the hurt on his face tore at her heart; she wanted desperately to take back every angry word she had hurled at him. She had no right to do that to him. "Oh, God," she whispered shakily. "I'm sorry." Somehow she had to find the courage to see this through. Hadn't she known all along that he had another destiny calling, deadlines to fulfill and demons to evade? She had no right to do this to him. He had made his decision, and their silent bargain had been that she would abide by it. She would not send him away with more guilt and regret; she did not want his last memory of her to be of a screaming, red-faced, tear-stained shrew.

"No, Jenny, I . . ." Once again he took an anxious half step toward her, but she warded him off with a lifted hand, turning from him, desperately struggling for control with an indrawn breath.

"No, you're right," she managed stiffly in a moment. "I—I knew from the first it—it couldn't last, and I can't keep you, if you don't want to stay."

"But Jenny, I—"

She shook her head tightly, silencing him. "I'm sorry . . . I said those things." Still she could not look at him. It was all she could do to keep her breathing even. "I had no right . . . to be angry with you. I know you have to do what you think is best, and—and you're right, there could never be anything more between us than . . . what we had. I didn't meant to spoil it with an ugly scene."

There was an endless, aching silence. She could feel his presence behind her; she could feel the weight of Bear's warm fur pressed anxiously against her leg. She knew Adam was waiting . . .

waiting for her to give him the freedom to leave without guilt, waiting for her to assure him that her memories of him would not be bitter, waiting once again to see the face of the woman he had loved. And she had to be strong enough to give him that. Somehow, she had to be strong.

At last she turned. It took every ounce of her courage to keep her face composed, and even, somehow, she managed a very weak, almost reassuring smile. "I'd like to know..." The calmness of her voice amazed her. She took a breath, and she thought she might just make it through. "What are you going to do? Have you decided?"

Something crossed his face. Anxiety? Hurt? Or perhaps just confusion and a measure of relief. His voice sounded dull, even though he, too, tried to smile. "I thought...Once you said... Well, writing is something I have the time for now, and it doesn't require a lot of physical strength. It gives you a kind of immortality, I guess and...I thought I'd give it a chance." He dropped his eyes. "Try to see the magic again."

An icy claw tightened abruptly around Jennifer's heart, but she said nothing. She stood, straight and still and dry-eyed, and waited for the moment when all that she loved and needed would turn and walk out the door.

Adam looked at her, and for just a moment the urgency and the need that flared in his eyes startled her pulse into a leap of hope. He said, "Jenny..." But that was all. His indrawn breath forced back the rest of the sentence, and he dropped his eyes. In only another moment he snapped his fingers and said abruptly, "Bear. Come."

The dog got to his feet and took a few steps toward Adam. Then, with an anxious whine, he came back to Jennifer and repeated the process, standing at last halfway between them and looking torn. Jennifer did not know how much longer she could hold back the tears.

Adam's eyes focused dully on the dog for a moment, and then he turned away. "Jenny," he said softly, so softly that she had to strain to hear. "I really do love you."

And the tears overflowed; there was nothing she could do to stop them. She pressed her fingers to her mouth, and it took more strength than she knew she possessed to keep herself from calling out to him. But this one thing she could do for him. She had to be strong enough to let him go....

He stood with his hand on the doorknob for what seemed like a very long time. She would hold that picture of him forever—his body poised to leave her and his muscles straining with reluctance, the dog standing halfway between them and looking back anxiously—her own tears blurring the scene into a hot-white etching of pain. And then he drew a sharp breath, his hand tightening upon the doorknob. "For God's sake, Jenny," he said hoarsely, "don't let me walk out this door!"

She flew to him and was crushed against his chest and lifted off her feet, her sobs lost in the warmth of his neck and the urgency of his mouth as it sought hers. For a long time they clung to each other, shaking breaths mingling into one, erratic heartbeats finding a single powerful rhythm, until at last their straining muscles loosened and desperate emotions calmed and they rested against each other, quiet in the confidence of their love.

"Oh, Jenny," he whispered, stroking her hair with an unsteady hand. "I never wanted to leave. It's taken all these weeks for me to get the courage to do it. I thought it was for the best ... I only wanted to do the best thing for you."

She shook her head slowly against his shoulder. "How could it be in my best interests for the only man I've ever loved to walk away from me? Adam ..." She pushed away from him, looking up at him with eyes dark with the nearness of her loss yet bright with the promise of the future. "Whatever happens, don't ever do that to me again. I can bear anything but that. Don't ever try to keep yourself away from me again."

Slowly, with exquisite tenderness, he bent his lips to her forehead. "I won't," he whispered. "Not ever again. And you promise me the same."

She nodded, the fear and concern evaporated into a crystal radiance of love that shone from her eyes so brilliantly it was almost blinding. "I promise."

Yet still there was the slightest trace of anxiety in his smile as he searched her face. "You might be sorry...."

"Never." Her voice was firm, and the love in her eyes opened the door to the future and revealed the certainty there. All he had ever wanted to see. Her hand slipped down his arm and closed around his. "Adam..."

Later, as they lay in the drowsy contentment of each other's arms, Jennifer turned to him, a slight uncertainty troubling her eyes. "Adam," she inquired softly, "will you be sorry? I know...how you feel about your deadline, and there was so much you wanted to see...."

He propped himself up on one elbow to look down at her. His hand moved with adoring delicacy over the features of her face, brushing her nose, her eyelids, tracing her lips, loving all of it. His eyes were clear and content. "No," he told her. "I won't be sorry. I knew a long time ago the only thing I ever wanted to see was you...." Happiness swelled within her like a multicolored bubble ready to burst as he cupped his hands about her face, his eyes alight with the wonder of it and deep with the certainty of his promise. "After all," he said softly, "you're the only one who's ever been able to make me see the magic, and when you have that, you don't need anything else."

Jennifer wrapped her arms around him and lifted her face to his, drowning in the embrace, only the first in a series of perfect moments—moments which, strung together one after another, could add up to a lifetime. That was all they needed, because when they were together, miracles were possible. No, they did not need anything else. Not anything at all.

Just what the woman on the go needs!

BOOKMATE

The perfect "mate" for all Harlequin paperbacks!

Holds paperbacks open for hands-free reading!

- TRAVELING
- VACATIONING
- AT WORK • IN BED
- COOKING • EATING
- STUDYING

Perfect size for all standard paperbacks, this wonderful invention makes reading a pure pleasure! Ingenious design holds paperback books OPEN and FLAT so even wind can't ruffle pages—leaves your hands free to do other things. Reinforced, wipe-clean vinyl-covered holder flexes to let you turn pages without undoing the strap...supports paperbacks so well, they have the strength of hardcovers!

Snaps closed for easy carrying.

Available now. Send your name, address, and zip or postal code, along with a check or money order for just $4.99 + .75¢ for postage & handling (for a total of $5.74) payable to Harlequin Reader Service to:

Harlequin Reader Service

In U.S.:
P.O. Box 52040
Phoenix, AZ 85072-2040

In Canada:
649 Ontario Street
Stratford, Ont. N5A 6W2

MATE-1